No one had ever kissed her like this. . . .

The kiss began gently. Ana shut her eyes and enjoyed the tenderness of his touch. Then, forgetting her anxieties, aware only of the moment and Brad's nearness, she kissed him more urgently. His touch became demanding, his grip on her arms tightened.

Ana felt her pulse jump. No one had ever kissed her like this. Sliding her arms around his neck, she pulled him even closer. Their bodies seemed to melt together, and Ana had no wish to pull back. Everything but Brad seemed far away.

Look for **BOYFRIENDS / GIRLFRIENDS** —the romantic series
by Katherine Applegate.

PARADISE

CHERYL ZACH

HarperPaperbacks
A Division of HarperCollins*Publishers*

HarperPaperbacks *A Division of* HarperCollins*Publishers*
10 East 53rd Street, New York, N.Y. 10022

Copyright © 1994 by Daniel Weiss Associates, Inc., and Cheryl Zach.
Cover art copyright © 1994 Daniel Weiss Associates, Inc.

All rights reserved. No part of this book may be used or reproduced in any manner whatsoever without written permission of the publisher, except in the case of brief quotations embodied in critical articles and reviews. For information address Daniel Weiss Associates, Inc., 33 West 17th Street, New York, New York 10011.

Produced by Daniel Weiss Associates, Inc., 33 West 17th Street, New York, New York 10011.

First printing: September 1994

Printed in the United States of America

HarperPaperbacks and colophon are trademarks of HarperCollins*Publishers*

10 9 8 7 6 5 4 3 2 1

One

....

"Dad, how could you do this to me?" Ana Puentes said. "I thought I could believe you this time." Brushing her long dark hair off her sticky forehead, she sighed with weariness and frustration.

The usual blare of announcements, multilingual chatter, and occasional radio music filled the large airport building. An older woman sitting across from Ana in a black plastic seat glanced Ana's way, then looked back to the two small children playing on the hard industrial carpet in front of her. A bearded young man in dark glasses two seats away had his head down almost to his chest, a gentle snore emerging from his half-open mouth.

But Ana's question went unanswered. Yet again, her father had failed to appear. Why was she surprised? It was the story of her life, Ana thought, feeling a spurt of anger and increasing impatience. Always a business meeting to attend, more important than his daughter's first ballet recital. Or an international call that took him out of the school auditorium just as she'd sung her big solo in the choir performance. Business had always come first with her father, and today was obviously no exception.

Her mother had warned her. "He'll probably be buried in work the whole time you're there, Ana," she'd said, standing in the foyer of their spacious Manhattan apartment. "Why waste your winter break? I thought you and Barry and Valerie and her friend had a ski trip planned. You worked hard last semester; have some fun on your vacation. Don't go all the way to Rio just to have your dad pull his usual stunt."

Her mother should know; her father's workaholic habits had brought about their divorce when Ana was thirteen. When the breakup came, Ana had left Brazil, returning to New York with her American mother, and had wondered bitterly if her dad would even notice that they were gone.

"But he asked me to come," Ana protested. "Dad wrote to me, asking me to spend some time with him. And besides"—she blinked hard to hold back the tears—"I can't go on the ski trip. Barry and I broke up last night."

"Oh, Ana, I'm sorry." Her mother put an arm around her shoulders. "I know it's no help now, but you're so young—there'll be other boys."

Ana shook her head. "Maybe. But I'm not going on the ski trip as a fifth wheel—Barry's already invited Nan Ragan to take my place—you see how brokenhearted he is. No, I'm going to Brazil, and Dad's going to keep his promise this time. I'm sure of it."

Now, sitting in the airport in Rio de Janeiro, Ana was anything but sure. She felt groggy from the long flight from New York, and her arm still ached from the shots her doctor had recommended. The air was hot and steamy. Maybe this whole trip had been a mistake.

But she'd been so moved when she'd received her father's letter. Pulling it from her overcrowded flight bag, she read it for the hundredth time, smoothing out the creases in the much-folded sheet of paper.

Dear Ana,

    On the day you turned seventeen, I called to wish you happy birthday. But you were out to dinner, the housekeeper said. I hope you got my message, and my card and gift.

I spent the whole day thinking how quickly time passes. Somehow, I thought you would be a little girl forever, with your sweet smile, soft hair, and beautiful green eyes. You used to look up at me with such love, I felt ten feet tall. I always knew, in the back of my mind, that I should spend more hours enjoying your company, but I thought there would be enough time later. Always I told myself that one of the reasons I was building up Puentes Industries was for you, so that I could give you everything you desired.

Now that you're nearly grown, I realize I wasted all those years when I should have been enjoying my baby girl, who is now almost a woman. I've realized that despite all the gifts and clothes and toys that I bought you, I deprived you of the greatest gift of all: a father who was there for you. And my heart grieves over mistakes I can't undo.

Can you ever forgive me, Ana? Will you give me another chance? Come to Rio after the holidays; I know you have some time off school for your winter break. Your mother has agreed, bless her, and if you will only come, I will try to make up to you, a little, for all the times I wasn't there.

Dear Ana, sweet daughter, please come.

With love,

Dad

The letter had meant so much to her. If her father had finally realized his mistakes, perhaps she could release the old anger she felt, blaming him for his long hours away at the office, his frequent business trips, blaming him even for the divorce. It had been almost two years since she'd seen him, during his last trip to New York—on business. Ana had looked forward to a real reunion, to time spent together getting to know her father from her vantage point as a young adult, not as a child.

He'd be surprised at how tall she was now—almost five seven—and at her maturing figure and thick dark hair, cut so that it curled softly around her cheeks. Most of all, she hoped he'd be impressed that she was learning to stand up for herself, to take care of herself.

They could explore Rio together, the city that Ana had once loved and now almost forgotten. Shutting her eyes for an instant, Ana searched for old memories. Strolling the black-and-white mosaic sidewalk along the Avenida Atlantica, sitting at an outdoor café enjoying *guaraná*, the sweet local soft drink, plunging into the surf lapping against a smooth, sandy beach—the images came back to her slowly.

How could she forget the salty tang of the ocean mingling with sweet aromas of tropical flowers? Or the cries of seagulls overhead while she sipped *água de côco* straight from a coconut or burned her tongue with spicy *feijoada*? And then there was the Cariocas' eternal good spirits, hearty enough all year, but especially frenzied during the parades and citywide parties of Carnaval, with its extravagant costumes and night-long celebrations.

It was her father who had taught her to sip green coconut milk from a straw inserted into the big nut. Ana sighed and checked her watch for the twentieth time.

And now he'd let her down again. She had a good mind to climb onto a plane and fly back to New York. That would show him. Deep down, Ana knew that being angry was better than admitting that tears lay all too close to the surface.

"Ana?" a male voice said. "Ana Puentes?"

Ana stiffened. It wasn't her father's voice. She stared at the dark-haired young man in the sleek business suit, fashionable and well-groomed enough to have just walked out of a Manhattan power lunch. His dark eyes were fringed by long lashes, and his handsome face had softened into a wide smile.

"Raoul?" she said. She stared hard to see the young man she had once played ball with, remembering his teasing her, humoring her, sometimes holding the ball over her head until the younger Ana yelled in fury. The skinny teenager she remembered had matured into dark Latin good looks; it took her a moment to recognize him. "I can't believe it's you—I haven't seen you since I was thirteen. How are you? How is your mother?"

"I am very well," he told her, bowing courteously over her hand. "As is Mama. She sends her fondest regards. You have changed so much, I hardly knew you. Welcome home, Ana."

"Thank you," Ana said, adding bluntly, "Where's my father?"

Raoul's smile faded to an expression of polite sympathy. "Your father has been delayed; he asked me to convey his regrets and to see you to the penthouse. You know I'm now employed by Puentes Industries as one of your father's executive assistants?"

Ana waved the information away, trying to control her almost overpowering disappointment. She blinked hard; she would not cry—she would not. But how dare her father stand her up, after that long letter that had seemed so sincere?

7

"He really couldn't help it," Raoul told her quickly, perhaps reading the turmoil of emotions in her face. "But he should be back in a few days. I will see to it that you are comfortable and not bored. There's much to do in Rio, after all."

Ana tried to force the bitter anger out of her expression. It wasn't Raoul's fault, but she was in no mood to be baby-sat, to be entertained by a polite family friend, even if they had played together years ago. And Raoul was certainly good-looking, but she just wasn't in the mood for a lighthearted flirtation.

"Where is my father? I have to speak to him."

"I'm afraid that's impossible," Raoul told her.

"Is he out of the country? You must have a phone number where he can be reached." First she would tell her father exactly what she thought of him, Ana told herself grimly. Then, after he knew how much he'd hurt her, breaking yet another promise just when she'd thought they had the chance for a fresh start, she would take off. She'd go back to New York and never set foot in Brazil again. Not even if he begged her. *How could I be so stupid as to be taken in by that letter? He didn't mean it. He didn't mean a word of it.*

Raoul smiled almost ruefully. "Actually, I don't. He's flown to the Amazon Basin, hundreds of miles from the city."

Ana's eyes narrowed. "What do you mean?"

"He's far upriver, deep in the rain forest. Phone communication is impossible."

Her city-bred tycoon father in the middle of nowhere? He never did anything like this. What was going on?

"Why?" Ana demanded. "He knew I was coming today. He promised just last week to be here to meet me. Why did he suddenly fly to the middle of the jungle?"

"It was a business emergency," Raoul told her, his dark eyes suddenly hooded as he glanced at his watch. "I don't know all the details. Please, let me take you to the penthouse. As soon as we have news of your father, I'll make sure you're the first to hear."

"Not good enough," Ana told him coolly, making up her mind with the same swift determination that had made her father so successful in his business.

Raoul looked surprised. "What do you mean?"

"There's no way I'm going to sit in his apartment twiddling my thumbs while he plays Indiana Jones and blows me off for the millionth time. He can't get away with it this time. I'm going after him, if I have to track him to the top of a rain-forest tree to do it."

Two

"But, Ana, you can't do that!" Raoul followed her through the crowded airport, brushing past women dressed in colorful dresses and sober business-suited men, raising his voice to be heard over static-blurred announcements of new arrivals.

Bustling ahead to claim the rest of her baggage, Ana ignored him. From the clamor of voices around her, at first almost unintelligible, words and phrases were emerging, as her own rusty Portuguese returned. Having made up her mind to a course of action, Ana was more relaxed. She smiled at a sudden memory, her prep-school roommate, Valerie, saying, "But I thought South Americans spoke Spanish."

"Most of them do," Ana had explained. "It all goes back to the first explorers. After Europeans

11

stumbled onto this 'new world,' the pope drew a line and divided it between Spain and Portugal; he didn't want two Catholic rulers warring against each other over new territories. He didn't know that Spain was getting the better deal, because they didn't know how big this continent was. But Portugal got Brazil, and that's why Brazilians speak Portuguese today."

Raoul's concerned voice broke into her thoughts. "Don't you understand? He's in the depths of the rain forest. It's practically impenetrable, and full of many dangers. Your father would not wish you to take such a foolhardy risk."

"Then he should have been here to tell me so himself," Ana said, her chin lifted stubbornly and her green eyes flashing. She grabbed her two other suitcases from the slow-moving carousel and dumped them at her feet. "Now, tell me his exact location."

"Ana, I do not want to see you in danger. And your father would be very angry." Raoul folded his arms.

"*I'm* very angry! He was supposed to be here—he promised. I didn't come here to sun myself on the beaches or party all night in the clubs—I came to see my *father*." Ana heard her voice rise and took a deep breath. It wasn't fair to yell at Raoul.

He looked at her now, his handsome face definitely troubled. Was he worried about his job? He had turned into a very good-looking man, she thought inconsequentially. Not quite her type—a little too smooth, somehow—but she could just imagine Valerie's reaction.

"Look," she said more gently. "I appreciate your concern. But no one will blame you; this is between me and my dad. I have to tell him what I think, face-to-face; then I'll go back to New York."

He looked into her eyes. "I'm begging you not to do this."

Ana stood resolutely before him.

Raoul sighed, shook his head. His tone was rueful. "Okay. I see you've inherited your father's stubbornness—but I knew that back when you were a little girl. If you've made up your mind, the best thing to do is to charter a plane. I can give you the coordinates of the small Puentes Industries airfield where your father flew to."

Ana took a deep breath, relief flooding her. "Thank you, Raoul."

He led the way to the counter where private planes could be chartered and spoke briskly to the woman behind the counter, setting up an immediate flight.

"Would you see to my luggage?" Ana asked.

"I'll just take my flight bag. I don't plan on staying long."

Raoul nodded. Twenty minutes later he was escorting her out on the hot black runway and handing her up the flight of folding steps to a very small chartered plane.

"Do be careful, Ana. The natives are fierce and uncivilized; some are headhunters. And the Amazon has dangerous animals and deadly diseases. It's not a pleasure spot."

Headhunters? It sounded very Hollywood; did Raoul have any real knowledge of the area, or was he as citified as her father? But Ana promised him she would take no chances. "I'll probably be back by tomorrow," she told him. "I appreciate your help, Raoul."

The fact was, her father would no doubt be angry at her for following him. Not to mention the fact that his business would keep him tied up, even in the rain forest. She'd probably be able to see him for only a short while. Would he be at all glad to see her? Perhaps Raoul was right, and she was making a mistake, barging in like this. But she'd had it. At least she'd be able to release some of her pent-up anger. Ana pictured a surprised greeting, then a big fight, then a chilly good-bye. Terrific.

But it was too late now. Ana had committed

herself, and there was no way she'd back down. Hurrying up the steps, she settled into a beat-up vinyl seat as the plane prepared for takeoff. The small plane had space for six; she was the only passenger. Through the small window beside her, she could see Raoul standing on the tarmac, frowning as if he still regretted letting her go like this.

I'll be careful, Ana told herself. She would get to see her busy father, if only for a few hours. She'd tell him exactly what she thought of his letting her down all over again. Then she'd come back to the city and take the next flight back to the States, tear up the letter, and give up on getting to know her father.

Besides the middle-aged, swarthy pilot, there was one other crew member, also a Brazilian, from the looks of him. After giving Ana friendly smiles and motioning for her to buckle her seat belt, they prepared for takeoff. The small motor roared to life with a surprising loudness, and Ana watched the ground slide swiftly past her window.

In a moment, she felt the plane lift free of the earth. But this ride wasn't like the one from New York. The small plane bounced and rocked with every shifting air current, and Ana found herself clutching the arms of her seat. And it was noisy;

the motor shrieked and whined, as though keeping them in the air were almost too much for its strength.

Her stomach lurched. Ana swallowed hard and dug into her backpack for her motion-sickness pills. Fortunately she still had part of a bottle of water that she had bought in New York. Unscrewing the cap, she popped the pill into her mouth and took a swig. By the time her rolling stomach had settled, the pill had also made her drowsy. Ana shut her eyes.

When she woke, the last vestiges of the city had been left far behind. The plane was flying over a leafy green blanket streaked by occasional ribbons of brown water. Sunlight dappled the vegetation with shadows as a few wispy clouds floated in the blue sky. The landscape looked peaceful and serene. Ana remembered Raoul's warnings—savage tribes, fierce animals, loathsome diseases. Looking down into the dense green jungle below her, she wondered for the first time if it did indeed hold these dangers.

Ana noticed that the green carpet of treetops was marred by occasional brown patches, ugly scars etched into the living green. She shivered.

"Senhorita Puentes?" The copilot had left his seat to approach her. "We shall arrive in about an hour," he told her in Portuguese. "It is a primitive airfield and has no radar, but no doubt we are the only plane in the area."

Ana thanked him, and he returned to the cockpit. What would her father say when she arrived unannounced and unexpected? Or maybe Raoul had sent a message ahead. He had claimed there was no phone communication, but unless Jose Puentes was out in the jungle itself, surely he'd have a radio at his camp.

Her father wasn't the adventurous type; she couldn't imagine any business crisis that would draw him into the rain forest. The Puentes business empire included factories, mines, and shipping lines, and her father had always kept a firm hand on every division of his diversified holdings. But though he often flew from one city to another, she couldn't remember his ever going into the jungle.

None of this made any sense, Ana told herself glumly. She'd hoped this trip would be fun—catching up on old times, getting to know her father, getting reacquainted with Rio—not chugging through the jungle. And yet the urge to see her father again was deeper and more intense than she liked to admit.

Her mother had rebuilt her own life after the divorce, filling her Manhattan apartment with friends of both sexes, jetting from New York to

Los Angeles to London to Paris, as the whim took her. She was always in the midst of a crowd, always with a meeting or a lunch or a party to go to.

Somehow in the midst of this unceasing activity, Alana Puentes designed expensive accessories; her whimsical scarves were sold in exclusive boutiques around the world. Her mother seemed to thrive on this frantic pace, but Ana sometimes thought of her mother as a reflection cast by a fast-moving car, the bright light receding even as she tried to grasp it.

True, Ana herself was away at school most of the year, but even on vacations Alana never seemed to slow down, and Ana missed having private time with her mother. Ana had unlimited credit cards and an ample allowance; what she didn't have was a family. She envied friends who had both parents at home, parents who could do things together, as a family. Without any brothers or sisters, with a busy mother and an absent father, Ana sometimes felt very alone. And now this breakup with Barry, her first serious boyfriend. . . .

Ana rubbed the crease of her tailored white shorts, detesting her momentary bout with self-pity. It wasn't as if she were homeless or dying of AIDS, she told herself. Plenty of people would be thrilled to change places with her. But still, she wanted to try one more time to forge a link with her father, to see if he had space in his life for his only daughter. It didn't seem too much to ask.

Sighing, she took a magazine from her bag and flipped through the pages. She found a candy bar in her purse, and with that and the bottled water, waited for the trip to end.

At last the plane dipped lower. Ana sat up straighter, checked her seat belt, and peered out the tiny window. At first she couldn't see any break in the tall trees—were they going to go down in the jungle itself? Alarmed, she thought of calling to the pilot, but then she saw the clearing, and some of her tension eased. But the airfield they were dropping toward was so tiny, it was impossible to relax completely.

Ana braced herself as the dirt field rose up to meet them. Then, with a bone-jarring bump, the plane bounced across the rough landing area. Ana held on tight to the arms of her seat, gasping as the plane finally rolled to a stop. "Talk about traveling rough," she murmured.

When the copilot came back to open the cabin door and unfold the steps, telling her she could step out of the plane, Ana had already picked up her pack.

He handed her a fresh plastic bottle of mineral water. "In case the facilities are not good," he said, nodding toward the rough airfield.

Ana thanked him, putting the water in her flight bag, then repeated her instructions to wait until she knew how long she would stay; transportation in this out-of-the-way part of the world was obviously not easy to come by.

She walked down the folding steps. The air felt thick enough to touch, warm and heavy with humidity. Waving one hand to dispel a cloud of buzzing gnats, she walked across the muddy field toward the tin-roofed, rough-walled hut that was the airfield's only building.

The door stood open. Ana stepped across the rough-hewn threshold and stared at the cluttered desk, the shelves of electronic equipment, and the man behind the desk, who yawned and stared at her suspiciously. He wore a tan shirt spotted with stains, and he needed a shave.

You were expecting Kennedy Airport? Ana thought as she prepared a polite smile and greeting.

"Boa-tarde," she told him, continuing in careful Portuguese. "Are you in charge here?"

The man stared at her as if she were an apparition out of the half-empty bottle on his desk. Hadn't he heard the plane land?

"I'm looking for Jose Puentes. He's my father."

The man blinked, looked dismayed. Surely he could understand her words, Ana thought. Her Portuguese might be rusty, but it couldn't be that bad. She had grown up in a bilingual family.

"*Compreende?* Do you understand?"

The man stroked his heavy mustache and sputtered a few words. His accent was strange, perhaps colored by native dialects, but after a moment, Ana understood it.

"I am in charge. Your father, he is in the forest, not here."

"But there is a way to get to my father's camp from here, yes? Raoul told me so."

"Raoul?" The man blinked again, then scratched his head. "Maybe, maybe . . ."

"No maybe about it," Ana told him. "I'll need a guide and a car, please."

"A car?" The man looked blank; then he laughed suddenly. "No, *senhorita* no car. But we'll find you a way to your father."

He stood up and left the small hut. Ana pushed a box off the nearest chair and sat down. The air in the room was hot and heavy with moisture; it smelled of stale cigarette smoke and cheap liquor. Great. This guy was a real prize, she thought, looking through the dirty window to the tall trees beyond. Still, it might not be easy to find men who wanted to work in the middle of the jungle.

She was relieved when the man returned, his frown replaced by a wide grin.

"I have a boat for you, Menina Puentes. Someone will take you upriver."

Of course, she should have realized she would travel by boat, Ana thought. She stood up quickly. "Thank you. My father will be grateful."

The man chuckled and rubbed his mustache again. "Oh, yes, *menina,* I'm sure."

Ana stared at him. What was she missing? His tone held more than polite obeisance to an employer's daughter. But she didn't have time to figure this out.

He pointed the way, and she picked up her backpack and followed him down a narrow path.

She would see her father soon. Yet as she picked her way carefully down the twisting trail, Ana felt a flicker of unease as tall trees blocked her view of the landing field.

For a moment, she wanted to run back to the plane, jump in, and fly quickly away. She felt trapped, as if she were losing her only way out.

Nonsense, Ana told herself.

But the airport chief leered back at her through the shadows, his expression ominous in the dim light. *"Tchau,"* he announced. "We part."

Three

Ana felt a stab of panic. Was he abandoning her? Then she realized that as they walked, the path and the forest floor had gradually sloped downward. The ground was becoming marshy; water seeped into the depressions left by her expensive sneakers. Now she saw the river just ahead, and a small boat awaiting her, with a dark-skinned, half-naked man sitting in the stern. The man beside her nodded to her guide in the boat, then stepped back.

"Thank you for your help," she told the airfield chief in Portuguese. "I'll be back tonight, tomorrow at the latest. Make sure that the plane waits for me."

The man nodded, chuckling a little beneath his breath as he headed back up the path.

This time, she ignored him. The man must be off his rocker—too much isolation and cheap booze, she told herself. She swung her pack into the boat, then stepped in carefully, feeling the sway of the craft as her weight moved it.

Quickly she crouched to take one of the rough seats. She gripped the sides of the vessel, trying to feel more secure. The boat seemed so small. But the river itself wasn't large. It was one of the countless tributaries of the Amazon, and a puny version of the great river itself, she guessed.

She looked over her shoulder at her guide, and the man stared back at her, unblinking. His dark hair was long and matted, his black eyes enigmatic. He was wearing the ripped and threadbare remnants of denim jeans, and nothing else; even his feet were bare.

"Olá, como vai?" she greeted him in careful Portuguese, but the man's broad features revealed no sign of comprehension.

She tried again. "We are going to my father's camp, yes? The camp of Senhor Puentes? You know the way?"

Still no response. Maybe he spoke only a native dialect. If he was from a native tribe, she couldn't guess which one. He could be one of the half-civilized part Indians who lived on the edge of society.

Ana swallowed, trying to keep her apprehension in check. Surely the airfield chief had explained her destination to the guide. But at this point, what choice did she have?

As if to illustrate her dilemma, the guide pushed the boat away from the bank. They moved into the center of the river as the whine of the boat's motor cut through the still air. The afternoon sun had dropped behind the tall trees, leaving the river cloaked in shadow. With the noon heat fading, the jungle seemed to be coming to life.

A high-pitched shriek made Ana jump; then she grinned nervously. That must be the call of monkeys high in the treetops; she also made out the whirl and hum of insect life and saw unexplained movement in the smooth surface of the river. She felt as if she had stepped into another world.

Manhattan was far behind her, with its noisy streets and sidewalks packed with people. Even Rio, cheerful and dirty and urbanized, was nothing like this. She felt grateful even for the company of the silent guide; he would know how to find her father's camp, then take her safely back to the airfield and her flight back to Rio.

She felt jittery only because this was all so different, Ana told herself. The ominous ripples in the murky river beyond, the grimy battered boat—it wasn't exactly a swan boat on the pond in Boston Commons, near her prep school.

Uneasily, she recalled all the dangers that Raoul had warned her about. Shaking her head to put them out of her mind, Ana tried to think positively. Later, when she was safely back at school, she'd tell Valerie the story, and they would laugh about how a monkey's shriek had made her jump.

The important thing was that this fragile-looking boat was taking her to her father. With any luck he would be pleased to see her, after all. Her own anger was fading, swamped by the barrage of new experiences she had encountered in the last several hours. Maybe their delayed reunion would be worth even this strange journey.

The air was thick and difficult to breathe; it smelled of the churned-up muddy water of the river, of the impossibly thick and verdant growth that surrounded them closely, and of the cloying sweetness of unknown jungle flowers that wove through the trees on clinging vines. Ana was grateful for the occasional breeze that cooled her face.

As the boat pushed its way through the water, Ana saw nothing except the thick twisting growth of native trees and shrubs. Even the river ahead of her was lost to view in the dim light. Occasional unexplained movements in the vegetation at the river's edge made her eyes widen, but the forest kept its secrets, and the inhabitants of this great wilderness seemed still in hiding.

At last they rounded a slight curve in the river, and Ana realized that the boat was definitely pointing toward shore, though she saw no sign of a landing pier. But the guide bumped the little boat into the tall plants at the river's edge, threw a rope around a tree root, and cut the engine.

She looked at him, but he only pointed toward the woods. Standing up, she balanced herself on the swaying boat and put her pack on her back.

But when she stepped out onto the muddy bank, the man sat unmoving in the stern.

"Aren't you coming to show me the way?" Ana asked, alarmed again. "How will I find the camp?"

His dark face could have been a mask; he made no response. She gestured at herself, at the forest, held up her arms, trying to act out her bewilderment.

But he only pointed once more toward the forest and grunted something that she couldn't understand.

Then, looking closer at the forest, she made out faint signs of a path, and some of her tension eased. The camp must be nearby; it would logically be close to the river and transportation. Surely someone at her father's camp would speak Portuguese, and she hoped she would find her father quickly and not have to make any long explanations to a stranger.

"All right, but you wait right here for me," she told him, gesturing emphatically at the boat and the landing spot, trying to make her meaning clear.

He stared back; it was like trying to talk to a stone pillar, Ana thought, frustrated. "You stay here, or my father will be angry," she told him sternly, trying to communicate with her tone if not her words.

Then, lifting her chin—she could hardly give up now, having come so far—she turned and walked into the forest. She marched quickly through the scattered trees. The rain forest was not as dense as it had looked at first glance, and the narrow path was easy enough to follow. The path was covered with a thin, slippery layer of fallen leaves. Against the brown padding, her footsteps made only a whisper of sound.

At first, the jungle around her seemed very quiet. As she walked farther, Ana heard faint rustles, impossible to identify or explain, though she strained to hear.

Her imagination, however, seemed to be working just fine. She pictured a hungry jaguar creeping up behind her, unheard until it sprang for her unprotected back, or giant snakes dropping out of the trees to wrap her in a life-ending embrace. She glanced around, stumbling as she tried to watch all sides at once. With her shoulders hunched tensely, she walked as rapidly as she could.

She was panting from her rapid pace by the time she glimpsed signs of the camp. There, through the trees, wasn't that the olive hue of a tent? Yes, and more portable buildings beyond. But the campsite seemed strangely silent. Were the men all out in the jungle right now?

Ana broke into a run, anxious to find another human being, one who could speak to her, explain the strange things that had been happening since her arrival in Brazil. Most of all, she wanted to find her father.

"Olá, olá!" she called. "Dad, are you here? Can anyone hear me?"

No answer. Frustrated, Ana stopped to look around at the camp. Walking to the nearest tent, she peered into the opening. Leaves had drifted onto the canvas floor. Inside, Ana saw a box with a jumble of canned goods, an overturned camp stool. Someone had been here, but the tent's inhabitants were nowhere to be seen.

Her apprehension growing, Ana glanced into two more tents, again finding no one, then walked toward the largest building. This was a lightweight portable structure with a canvas roof and walls. A screen door marked the entrance.

"Olá?" Ana called once more, hoping beyond hope for a rational explanation to this additional puzzle. Hesitating only a moment, she pulled opened the light door and walked inside.

Her spirits revived instantly. Behind a small portable table littered with papers, a pudgy man in khaki clothes slumped in his chair in a normal afternoon siesta, a broad-brimmed straw hat covering his face. At last, someone who could tell her where her father had gone, how soon he would return.

"Olá?" Ana called more loudly. She crossed the short distance to stand over him. "Excuse me, but—"

The odor was the first warning; the foul smell made her put up one hand to block her nose. Then she looked down and saw a thick stream of ants marching unheeded up the trousered leg of the stranger.

Ana felt goose bumps rise on her skin and stepped backward, gasping. When she raised her eyes, she saw the stains on the dark khaki shirt that she had missed at first—heavy brownish stains, with flies buzzing over them. Dried blood? There was no rise and fall of the chest beneath the shirt. The man's jaw, the only part of his face showing beneath his hat brim, looked distended and swollen.

The stranger wasn't asleep. He was dead.

Ana felt paralyzed with fear and repulsion. Shuddering, she backed slowly away until the thin mesh of the screen door touched her back. Pushing the door open, she ran out of the canvas hut.

Stumbling on the rough dirt outside, Ana fell, landing hard on hands and knees. The jolt of the fall shook her, but she had more trouble controlling her heaving stomach. She fought back the sour taste of her fear, then scrambled to her feet, still trembling.

Who was the dead man? Of the few men she remembered from her father's business empire, no one matched the body's shape and size.

More important, who had killed him? Was the killer still lurking behind a canvas flap in one of the tents she hadn't checked, or standing just outside the clearing, watching her from behind a tree?

She couldn't stay here. If only her father would come striding out of the jungle, his arms open wide, a smile on his face. Ana prayed for his safety, even as she wished for the comforting strength of his presence. Not until this moment did she realize just how much she'd wanted to see him again. Past the anger, the resentment, the need for her father's love and protection remained. But there was no way she could stay in this place of death and horror.

She had to get back to the airfield, and if the man there had no better answer for her, she would fly back to Rio—no, to the nearest large town, and contact Raoul. He would help her find her father. It was the wisest course, the only choice.

"So why do I feel like a coward, as if I'm running away?" Ana muttered, pushing back a strand of damp brown hair that had fallen into her face.

There was, of course, no answer. The camp lay silent around her, a dead man its only occupant. At least, she hoped she was alone.

Telling herself that she was not fleeing blindly, Ana ran down the path, back to the river and the boat. The path seemed longer this time; she thought she'd never see the glint of water beyond the forest. Her flight bag was heavy over her shoulder, and her purse slapped against her side as she loped through the jungle. Her stomach twisted with anxiety and fear, and she found it hard to catch her breath.

At last the path took one last bend, and she heard the slight sound of water lapping against the bank.

Finally, she had reached the river. She would be grateful to see even her morose guide. Anyone human would be a comfort to her now.

Her chest heaving, sticky perspiration clinging to her forehead, Ana emerged from the trees. She glanced wildly at the riverbank. Tall grasses swayed in the slight breeze, and a bird called, hidden inside the tangled water plants.

But the boat was gone.

Four

It was a nightmare. It couldn't be true. The boat *had* to be around here somewhere. It simply had to be. Forcing herself to take a deep breath, Ana tried to push back her fear.

For a moment she wondered if she'd somehow come out of the forest at the wrong place on the river. Maybe she'd strayed from the path as she ran, or had somehow taken a different branch.

But there'd been no other pathway, not that she had seen. Looking now, she could see fifty yards or more of the river, and there was no small boat anywhere along the bank, no matter how hard she strained her eyes.

Besides, moving closer to the water's edge, she could see grasses trampled down on the muddy bank, and even her own footprint where she had stepped off the boat. This was the right place. And the boat was really gone.

She'd been abandoned. She was alone in an unknown rain forest, with no sign of any other living being. Where was her father, and the other men from the camp? Had the camp been attacked by some warlike native tribe, as Raoul had warned her? Had her father been taken captive? Suddenly, corny Hollywood jungle movies, with their cartoonish depictions of headhunters, and even cannibals, rushed into her mind. Cannibals?

This was impossible. Ana felt as if she'd wandered into a time warp. A dim memory of old headlines returned. There were also smugglers in the rain forest. What about the drug lords of Colombia, northwest of Brazil? Drug cartels might exist in other South American countries, too, and no one could be more brutal. Could they have some connection with her father's camp?

She was guessing wildly. Ana told herself sternly to stick to the facts. But what were the facts? A dead body lay in the camp behind her, mute testimony to her danger. Her guide and her only means of escaping the jungle were gone. Her father was nowhere to be found. Only Raoul had some idea of her whereabouts, and he was back in Rio.

Ana felt exposed; she could feel tightness in the small of her back, as if unknown eyes might be watching. Plan—she needed a plan. For just a moment she sank onto a fallen log crossing her path. Hungry mosquitoes and gnats buzzed annoyingly around her head; she brushed them away.

Okay. First thing to do was get out of sight, make herself less vulnerable. Who knew what was lurking in the jungle, or lying in wait for her? Second, she must find her way back to the airfield, the chartered plane, and then to civilization and help. But how, without the boat?

For an instant, Ana felt suffocated. Terror lay like a weight against her shoulders, her chest, pressing her down. She had to get out of there, get moving, even if she didn't know where to go.

Back into the trees she ran, several hundred yards through the forest, until some sanity returned. She stopped and tried to catch her breath.

Away from the river, she felt foolish. She couldn't go on like this; she'd be lost in minutes. Clearly, the river would lead her back to the airfield. Of course the journey would take much longer by land than by water, but the river would take her in the right direction, and then she could get help.

In the meantime, if there were savage natives in the forest, how on earth could she avoid them? They were at home here and could be silent and hidden if necessary. Whereas she was conscious of every rustle she made, every tree she bumped into, the loud rasping of her breath in the heavy, sodden air.

Now Ana wished that she were more familiar with her birth country. Despite living in Brazil for thirteen years, she'd never had any great interest in the rain forest. Her only knowledge of it came from recent television specials and fund-raising concerts. She shivered, remembering an article about the brightly colored little frogs whose skin oozed poison used for blow darts and fine arrows. Biting her lip, she glanced around her fearfully, as if waiting for the prick of a silent barb that could come without warning from any direction.

On the other hand, the man in the camp looked as though he had died from bullet wounds. No arrows had been sticking out of the body. And no headhunter had taken his trophy, complete with straw hat, home. Were there still headhunters? Ana wished she knew.

But now she had a long trek ahead of her, and the sun would soon set. The boat ride had taken the better part of an hour, and Ana wondered how that translated into walking time. It would be slow going through the jungle, stepping carefully over vines, going around thick-trunked trees, watching carefully for snakes, spiders, and other insects. Squaring her shoulders, Ana had to face the fact that she might not reach the airfield before dark. The thought of a night spent alone in the wilderness made her stomach knot, and a cold sweat broke out on the back of her neck. Still, the longer she hesitated, the later she'd arrive at the airfield.

She refused to consider that she might never get there—that another fate awaited her inside the forest. Blind fear would only follow that thought, and unchecked panic would lead her to destruction.

Lifting her chin again, Ana slipped her thumb under the strap of her flight bag to lighten her load, and set out toward the river. She retraced her steps until she reached its edge, then started downriver along its banks.

But it was harder to follow the river than she had expected; the water often seeped over the banks to cover the forest floor, forcing her to detour around flooded areas. Once she considered simply sloshing through the marsh, since the water didn't appear deep there.

But as she debated, a rustle of sound made her

turn. The dark rippled body of an alligator, more than six feet long, slithered into the water, then swam a few feet and turned. Lying barely submerged, the gator pointed its long head toward her, its beady eyes bright.

Shuddering, Ana backed away, giving up any thoughts of wading through the swamp. She made her way around the water-logged forest, eventually coming back to drier ground. This time, trying to stay alert without seeing natives behind every tree, she paid more attention to the rain forest itself.

The trees stretched straight up; their leafy tops towered thirty or forty feet above the forest floor. Their green canopy of heavily leafed branches caught most of the sunlight; it was amazingly dim where Ana stood, even in the afternoon. The filtered light hung like a golden cloud, blurring the outlines of the tall trees. Many of the forest giants had wedgelike buttresses protruding from their trunks, but underbrush was scarce, so it was easy enough to pick her way through the dim forest without a path.

Her flight bag seemed to grow heavier with every step. Frequently, she wiped large drops of perspiration off her forehead. The air was heavy with moisture; she could feel it brush her face like a damp curtain. The forest was so quiet that she could hear herself panting as she walked. Ana strained to hear the sound of any footsteps behind her.

The occasional shriek of a monkey from overhead made her start, but though she once saw leaves rustle, the animals swung unseen in the top layer of the treetops. She seemed alone down below. Where were all the animals? On the other hand, Ana reflected, she didn't really want to know.

She stepped aside to avoid the heavy loops of vinelike plants that covered some of the trees. A fallen tree trunk blocked her path; perhaps she could sit and catch her breath. She inspected the greenish-white bark for snakes or insects, brushed off a bit of fungus, and sat down. But the log crumbled beneath her, dumping her into the dirt.

"Hey!" Ana looked at the log and saw that the apparently solid surface was as fragile as glass. Beneath the thin bark the wood was honeycombed with tunnels filled with industrious lines of whitish insects. Ants?

"Termites, dummy," Ana told herself. But there could be ants, too. She scrambled to her feet, brushing off her once white shorts, wincing as she felt the result of the fall.

Giving up any idea of sitting, she marched on,

pausing only to finish her New York water and start on her Brazilian mineral water. She rationed it, not knowing how long it would have to last her. After another hour, her too-new sneakers had begun to rub the little toe on her right foot. She would soon have a beaut of a blister. Ana considered stopping again; she thought she had a bandage in her bag. But every time she paused, she could feel eyes on her back, almost hear the sounds of pursuit.

Probably just her imagination. If she'd been followed from the abandoned camp, surely her pursuers would have attacked by now. If they wanted to kill her, when would they have a better chance? Ana shuddered at the thought.

How far had she come? Was she still headed in the right direction? Ana realized she hadn't seen the river in some time; her last detour had taken her a considerable distance inland.

If only she could see the sun, she thought. She was sure the airfield was due east, but the thick layers of leaves overhead blocked the sunlight so thoroughly, she couldn't be sure of her bearings.

Despite the delay, she'd better try to find the river again, make sure she traveled in the right direction. As long as she headed downriver, she'd be okay. Ana turned to the right and cautiously headed for the river.

A clump of green-and-white flowers on a tree trunk attracted her attention; she'd seen few blossoms in this otherwise lush forest, though their scent often drifted toward her in the thick air. As Ana drew closer, she blinked in surprise. The "flowers" suddenly separated and flew away—as large, beautifully marked butterflies.

Nothing here was what it seemed.

A rustle in the trees beyond made Ana forget about flowers. She stood very still. Was it the murderer, tiring of the pursuit at last? Had an Indian tracked her silently all this time?

Yet surely a native would not make so much noise. An animal, maybe a jaguar? Or an anaconda, the snake that grew big enough to swallow a deer? The sound came again. Ana looked about wildly, searching for anything to use as a weapon. There were no rocks on the forest floor, only a thick layer of fallen leaves. There—a portion of a fallen tree branch.

She grabbed the piece of wood and lifted it, her arms raised, ready to strike.

With a sudden explosion of movement, the animal emerged from behind a tree. She saw a low, heavily rounded body trotting on brown stubby legs. Gasping, Ana hit at the creature.

The limb snapped easily in two, and the animal—piglike, but with a tapered snout—changed direction and ran off, squealing in alarm.

It was a tapir; Ana remembered the animal from zoo visits. Harmless, surely, but her heart still thudded violently. Trying to catch her breath, she stepped away, thankful that her fear had been for nothing.

And backed into a warm, breathing body.

Ana screamed.

The sound seemed to echo beneath the trees, filling her ears in a weird, dreamlike way. Whirling, she gasped, too horrified to scream again.

It was a man, and he was close enough to reach out and grab her. Desperately, she wanted to run but couldn't seem to make her legs work.

Then a few details started filtering into her panicked mind. He was a few inches taller than she, and young, though it was hard to tell in the gloom. His skin was bronzed and bare above a dirty pair of khaki shorts, and his longish dark hair was held back by a faded bandanna. Mud-caked sneakers covered his feet, and his broad shoulders were braced against the weight of a worn, nondescript backpack. A wicked-looking machete was in one hand.

His expression was grim. And he had startling blue eyes.

Blue?

A half-native? A drug smuggler, who would kill her as easily as spitting a fish from the river?

Ana licked suddenly dry lips and decided to try a short phrase in Portuguese. *"Olá. Me chamo senhorita Ana Puentes. Como se chama?"*

The stranger stared. Either he didn't understand, like the boat guide, or he was interested neither in her name nor in identifying himself. The silence was so thick with tension that Ana found she was holding her breath; her whole body was stiff. Far away, she heard a bird chatter. She thought of running, but her knees felt weak; she was afraid she'd collapse if she took a step. Anyhow, how far could she get?

"Fala Português?" She tried once more, but if he did understand Portuguese, he made no answer. His expression, if anything, looked even more menacing.

There were hundreds of Indian dialects, and she knew none of them. She held out her hands, palms upturned; she had seen the gesture in a movie.

"Please, I mean no harm," she told him in English, desperate to communicate.

"Since you couldn't do much damage with your little purse, it's just as well, isn't it?" the stranger said clearly.

Ana was so astonished, she couldn't answer. Her green eyes widened. A quick surge of relief was replaced quickly by anger.

"Why didn't you say you speak English? Who are you?"

Five

Dark brows raised, but the brilliant blue eyes didn't blink.

"My name is Brad Eliot." His English held no trace of a Portuguese or native accent; in fact, she thought it sounded American, with a faint British overlay.

"Are you American? What are you doing here?" she asked.

"I could ask the same of you." He looked her up and down almost in derision.

Feeling curiously defensive, Ana looked down at her dirty tailored linen shorts and fashionable knitted top. Her purse was leather and expensive, from a limited designer series. So?

Her initial wave of relief was fading; now some of her suspicion returned. Just because he spoke

English didn't mean he wasn't a criminal. She was suddenly unsure about how much to tell him. What if he had been involved in the murder? If he knew she'd seen the dead man, she'd be dangerous to him. And someone who'd murdered once wouldn't hesitate to do it again.

"I asked first," she said childishly, the events of the day straining her self-control almost to the very limits.

He grinned, but his eyes were cool. "My mother has a camp downriver," he told her calmly. "I live here."

It was the last answer she had expected. Was he really part native after all? But his English was so good . . . and his features betrayed no trace of an Indian background. Calmly, as though he had run into her in a city park one afternoon, he turned away and prepared to disappear back into the jungle.

"Wait!" she called in alarm. "I need help."

"The Puentes camp is that way." He pointed, but didn't slow his stride or look back.

Ana bit her lip, then threw dignity to the winds and ran after him. The thought of being alone again in the jungle made her want to scream, and the sunlight was fading rapidly.

"You don't understand," she told him, following the broad shoulders visible under the ancient backpack, the tanned skin and supple muscles coated with a light sheen of perspiration. She had to take quick steps to keep up with him. "I need someone to guide me back to the airfield. My boat and guide left without me."

He shrugged. "Get one of your father's goons; he has plenty on the payroll."

"I can't! Please don't leave me. I'm—I'm lost."

This time he glanced over his shoulder. "Look, if a spoiled, rich city girl wants to come and play in the jungle, it's not my fault if she can't follow her own trail. I told you, the camp is that way."

Biting back angry words, Ana took a deep, calming breath. Brad Eliot was the only person she had seen all day who could speak English, and who could possibly help her out of this awful predicament. She needed him; she needed his help.

"Please, just help me get to the airfield," she repeated calmly, struggling to keep her voice even. "I'll pay you."

He gave her another sardonic glance but didn't slow his pace. "I don't need your money, and I have more important things to do. Get another guide. I told you, go back to camp."

Her self-control snapped. "I can't go back there," she blurted. "No one's there. My father's missing—I don't know where he is. And someone's dead. There's a body—" She stopped, aghast at having told him so much.

He stopped so suddenly that she almost bumped into him again. Turning, he gave her his full attention.

"What do you mean, body?"

Ana held her breath, but she couldn't take back what she'd said. More words tumbled out, but she struggled to tell her story clearly.

"I flew here today from Rio to find my father. A man in a boat brought me from the airfield to my father's camp and left me. But no one's at the camp, and I don't know where my father's gone. In one of the huts, there's a . . . a dead man. I don't know who he is or why he's dead. Now I just want to go back to Rio to look for my father. I need to get to the airfield!" She was horrified to hear her voice break on a sob. Taking a deep breath, she shut her eyes for a moment. She would not fall apart in front of this unsympathetic stranger.

When she opened her eyes, he was still watching her, his expression hard to read.

"I'll take you back to the camp."

"No!" She almost stamped her foot. "Didn't you hear me—there's no one there. There's a plane waiting for me at the airfield. I have to go back. I need help to find my father—something may have happened to him." She tried to speak slowly and clearly, as though explaining the situation to a child—or to an idiot.

"Look," Brad told her, his voice level. "The airfield's the other way, and I don't have any time to waste."

What a jerk! "Please," Ana said, using every ounce of willpower she had to remain calm. "Finding my father is very important. He could be hurt, injured, or . . ." Her mind couldn't dwell on the horrible possibilities.

"You don't know for sure your father's in danger," Brad pointed out maddeningly.

"There's a dead man in camp!" Ana snapped.

"So you say." Those dark brows lifted again; he was the most infuriating person she had ever met.

"Are you saying you don't believe me? Do you think I'm making this up?"

"Let's just say I want to see for myself. And anyhow, the camp's only a mile away."

A mile! But she had been walking for hours! Groaning inwardly, Ana realized she had been going in circles. But seeing Brad walking away, she hurried to follow. The idea of seeing the body again made her feel frightened all over, but she wasn't about to be left alone to wander in the jungle until she collapsed from exhaustion.

They reached the camp within half an hour,

Ana walking swiftly to keep up with Brad's rapid pace. The olive-colored tents looked just as they had at her first visit. Everything was still deathly quiet, Ana thought, then wished for another adverb.

Silently, she pointed to the large canvas hut, and waited outside while Brad went in to investigate.

It seemed a long time till he pushed open the screen door, but it was probably only minutes. When he came out, his expression was hard.

"There. Now do you believe me? He's dead, isn't he? I told you." Ana was aware of sounding petulant, but no longer cared.

"There's no one in there—alive, dead, or otherwise," Brad said, his voice tight with anger.

"What?" Unbelieving, Ana ran into the tent to see for herself.

The portable table still sat in the center of the tent, and a folding chair behind it had been overturned. But there was no body, no sign of any human being. Ana didn't trust her own eyes. Venturing closer, she caught just a whiff of the foul smell of death she had noted earlier. So she hadn't dreamed the dead man. The body had been moved, and very recently. Ana felt her skin crawl.

This meant the murderer, or murderers, could be anywhere. Suddenly she saw a large rent in the back of the canvas wall; it hadn't been there be-fore.

Brad stepped into the tent behind her; she felt rather than saw his presence. Was it Brad, after all? Had he had time to slit the canvas and haul the body out to a hiding place while she waited unknowingly outside? She stood stiffly, very much aware that he was just behind her. Was he lifting the machete, ready to dispose of an incon-venient witness?

When he touched her shoulder, she jumped, crying out in alarm.

But when she whirled to face him, he looked as surprised as she. "Hey, relax. I told you, there's nothing here."

"There was," she told him grimly.

He reached for her, and she choked back a cry, retreating instinctively. But he caught her, his grip alarmingly strong, held her by the arm, and reached for her with his other hand, his machete tucked into his belt.

Ana felt frozen with fear.

Brad touched her cheek lightly, then her fore-head. "You don't feel feverish," he murmured. "Are you taking your malaria pills?"

"I don't need pills; I need you to listen to me," Ana said, feeling as though she had wandered into a horrible nightmare not of her own making.

She felt that she would give anything at that moment to be killing time in the airport in Rio, fuming over her father's absence, rather than here in the jungle, fearing his death. "I didn't dream it," Ana said slowly. "I know I didn't." She stepped back, and he dropped his hands. "There was a body here. Look."

She pointed to the table, to the dark brownish stains that covered several sheets of paper.

Brad nodded. "It looks like blood. But there could be lots of explanations—"

"I tell you, I saw the body! He was dead."

"Did you take his pulse?"

Reluctantly, Ana shook her head. "I didn't want to touch him."

"So he was probably just asleep."

"The body was bloated. And the smell . . ." She shuddered. "It was awful."

"City girls have delicate noses." Brad almost grinned. "He could have been sick, in a coma, even, and someone moved him after you left."

Shaking her head, Ana said softly, "There were ants crawling up his leg." Looking around on the floor, she saw them, still swarming in confused black lines. "See?"

Brad looked down and saw the ants. He frowned and rubbed his chin.

"Where are all my father's men who should

54

be here? And where's my father?" Ana asked, not really expecting this person to answer. All of a sudden she felt weary and hopeless. She was filthy, hungry, lost. . . . Weakly she moved toward the door.

Turning on his heels, the stranger preceded her out the door. Ana followed him outside the tent.

"Where are you going?"

"To check the other tents."

Nervously, Ana followed, watching him plunge into the smaller tents set around the clearing. But he found no inhabitants, and he was frowning as he emerged from the last one. "No one here."

Like I've been telling you. "Now will you please take me to the airfield?" Ana asked, hoping that she had convinced him at last.

"I told you, I have more important things to do."

Ana wanted to scream but tried to keep her voice reasonable. "More important than helping me get help, so I can find my father, who could be in serious danger?"

"Frankly, yes," he told her steadily. "There are children ill, even dying, in a village some miles from here. I have medicine to deliver, and it's perishable. I've already lost over an hour because of your overactive imagination. Look, there are supplies here; your father and his crew might be back soon, maybe even tonight. If not, just wait here till I return, and I'll take you to the airfield then."

Ana's shoulders slumped. "There was a dead man here. What if his murderers come back?" she asked. She grabbed his arm, trying to hold his attention. "I'm a witness—what do you think they'll do to me? Besides, I'm worried sick about my father—I know he must need help."

"Your father creates danger; he's an aggressor, not a victim."

"What in the world does *that* mean? What's wrong with my father?"

His expression was hard, revealing little. Ana gritted her teeth as he turned toward the jungle again.

"Please! You can't leave me here!" Ana thought quickly. "Look, if you take me back to the airfield, I'll hire a plane for you. You could fly to the village in an hour. Even with the detour, you'd get there faster than going by foot."

He paused, but only for a moment. "There's no airfield where I'm going."

"I'll get you a water plane," she told him desperately. "Or a helicopter. There's a radio at the airfield; we can call for what we want. I have all the money we'd need."

"No doubt," Brad said dryly. "How do I know you'll keep your promise?"

"How do I know you'll keep yours?" she re-torted. "I always keep *my* promises, Brad Eliot!"

He considered, meeting her eyes for a long moment, then nodded slowly. "All right."

Her victory brought relief so overwhelming that she felt her head spin. She wavered, and Brad grabbed her arm again to steady her.

"When did you last eat?"

Ana tried to think. Breakfast on the plane from New York—or was that yesterday? "I don't know. I've been traveling almost twenty-four hours."

"There are supplies here. Let me see what I can find."

"No, don't worry about it," Ana said quickly. "Let's just get out of here. I'll be fine."

Brad looked up at the sky, judging the setting of the sun. "It's about to get dark anyway. We might as well eat now—I'm not about to carry you if you pass out from hunger," he told her. "And traveling at night isn't practical. If I'm stuck with you, it's better that we stay here where there's some shelter, then head out at dawn."

Ana wanted to argue. What if the killer re-turned? But she suddenly realized she was so tired that she could hardly stand. "Okay."

While Brad looked for something to eat, Ana found the latrine. Coming out, she located a bucket of water and tin basin and washed her hands and face. Her water bottle had been empty for some time, and she eyed the water in the pail, wondering if it was safe. It looked clear enough, though it was hard to see in the rapidly fading light. Her mouth and throat ached with dryness. She cupped her palm and raised the tepid liquid to her mouth.

"Stop!" Brad's call was sharp.

Startled, Ana let the water fall. He stood behind her, coming up as quietly as a jungle cat.

"Don't drink that—it's from the river. Don't you know anything about the tropics?"

Ana felt her cheeks redden; she hated looking stupid. But the answer to his question was obvious.

Brad shook his head at her ignorance, then motioned her to another tent, lifting the mosquito netting at the entrance to allow her to bow her head and step inside. A small lantern provided light, and he had opened cans and heated the contents on a small propane stove. He handed her a liter of bottled water, and Ana drank thirstily before gulping down the canned stew. She swallowed it so fast she hardly tasted it; she hadn't realized she was hungry.

"You didn't answer my question earlier. Have you taken your pills today?" Brad ate from his own can, sitting Indian-style across from her on the canvas floor of the tent.

"Pills?" Ana repeated blankly.

"Malaria, worm, you know."

"Worms?" Ana felt her throat close and put down the almost empty can.

Brad frowned, then went to a box of supplies set against the tent wall. Rummaging through the contents, he brought her a selection of bottles and jars.

"Take one of these a day," he told her. "And put the insect repellent on any bare skin." He looked down at her legs.

Following his gaze, Ana bit her lip. Her legs were scratched and muddy from her scramble through the jungle. Even so, she suddenly felt exposed. His eyes glinted; then he looked away. She thought she must have imagined his brief change of expression.

She sniffed the jar, wrinkling her nose at the odor of the insect repellent. "I haven't been bitten too badly yet," she said defensively.

"Listen, you idiot, what do you think the most deadly animal in the jungle is?" Brad sat back on his heels and regarded her steadily.

"Jaguars?" she guessed.

Brad snorted in derision. "They're almost extinct, thanks to people like your father." He went on quickly, before Ana could interrupt in angry defense. "The most dangerous killers here are diseases, and most are carried by insects, like mosquitoes. You can die in two days or twenty years, from a variety of nasty ailments. Trust me—your life depends on this. Use the insect repellent, take your pills, and don't drink any water that's not bottled, boiled, or chemically treated."

Ana looked at the bottles in her lap. The pills were labeled in Portuguese, and she strained her eyes in the dim light to read the label. How did she know he was telling the truth? These pills could be anything.

Brad's grin was twisted. He took one of the pills and tossed it into his mouth, gulping it down with a swallow of water. "See? No cyanide."

He didn't have to be such a mind reader, Ana thought resentfully. She swallowed a pill from each bottle and waited for any reaction, but felt nothing, except a new wave of fatigue.

Brad found a string hammock for her and showed her how to hang it from the tent posts.

"Maybe it would be better if I just slept on the ground," Ana said, eyeing the thin hammock with distrust. "If I turn over in my sleep, I'll fall out."

"Then you'll learn not to turn," Brad answered, with no sign of sympathy. "It's the best way to sleep here. Unless, of course, you're not worried about snakes or poisonous insects."

Beaten, Ana wearily wrapped a blanket around

herself—the air had cooled quickly after dark—and climbed cautiously into the hammock.

Watching her with grim amusement, Brad told her, "I'll be in the next tent. Call me if you see any more dead bodies. Or if you don't."

"Don't hold your breath." She glared at him, but Brad only grinned and lifted the mosquito netting to step out of the tent.

No way would she admit how gorgeous she thought he was, not with his attitude. Why wouldn't he believe her? She hadn't dreamed the dead man; a killer still lurked in the rain forest. She'd never be able to sleep, between the terrors outside and the strange feel of the hammock. She thought about how her mother must be worrying. Ana hadn't called home from the airport, as she'd promised. She hadn't wanted to admit that her father hadn't shown up. Ana felt a stab of guilt, thinking of her mother's anxiety. She would contact her mom as soon as she got back to civilization, Ana told herself.

She shut her eyes, ready to wait out a long night.

When she opened them again, daylight was filtering through the canvas walls of the tent.

Sleepily she blinked her eyes, then stretched her arms overhead. Instantly the hammock shifted and she promptly fell out, landing with a grunt on the hard floor of the tent.

"Ouch!" She stood up carefully, rubbing a sore elbow, as memories flashed back. The unscheduled flight to the Amazon, the empty camp, the dead body—that man *had* been dead, no matter what Brad said. At least today she could fly out of this awful wilderness, get help to find her father, get back to civilized society.

Eager to get going, she ran a comb through her hair, drank some bottled water, and gulped down the pills Brad had prescribed. Then she put the bottles in her purse, along with the rest of the water. Bending over, she hastily smeared the foul-smelling insect repellent all over her dusty legs. It stung where she was scratched, and she gritted her teeth. Soon she would smell so bad, nothing with a nose would come near her.

Next she peeled off her socks, wincing at the blisters on her sore feet. Rummaging through the little cupboard in the tent, she found some antibiotic cream. After these rituals, she put her head outside the tent; no one was in sight. None of her father's men seemed to have returned to the camp. Especially not her father.

Leaving her tent, she glanced around for Brad, but he too was nowhere to be seen. Was he still asleep? Ana looked at the tent next to her own. "Brad?"

No answer. Ana approached the tent, hesitated, then made up her mind. She didn't want to waste any more time. "Brad, are you in there?"

She lifted the tent flap. The tent was empty. A quick surge of panic clutched Ana's throat. Had he abandoned her to the dangers of the jungle and the unknown killer? Had he been lying about their agreement? Her breath coming quickly, Ana looked around the small tent. No, there was his knapsack. At least, it looked like the one he'd been carrying. She almost gasped with relief.

She bent closer to inspect it, wanting only to reassure herself that her mysterious guide would be back. The first thing she saw was another faded bandanna, like the one Brad wore to hold his hair out of his eyes. Yes, this was Brad's knapsack.

A folded sheet of paper lay beneath the bandanna; Ana eyed it, struggling with her conscience. This was certainly prying. On the other hand, someone in this jungle was a killer. It would help to know that it wasn't her guide. Just how much did she know about him, anyway? More information would be reassuring. Ana pulled out the paper, unfolded it, and scanned it quickly.

It was a map, a map of the jungle, with some Polaroid photos clipped to the lower edge. The pictures showed jungle with bare ground where digging had begun; the markings on the map told her little. Then she noticed the name at the corner of the sheet—Puentes Mining Company.

As she gripped the buff-colored sheet in suddenly rigid fingers, a picture formed in her mind as a memory returned. A map like this one had lain on the portable table in the main tent the first time she had entered, when she'd discovered the body. Ana realized now that it had been missing the second time she'd entered the tent.

She inspected the paper more carefully and noticed several dark stains on the bottom half. Dried blood? Her stomach turned, and she felt almost sick with fear.

Six

Ana clutched the map, feeling paralyzed. She tried to decide what to do. If Brad was the killer, she couldn't go back into the jungle with him—he might murder her, too.

Get a grip, Ana told herself. *If he'd wanted to get rid of you, he could have killed you last night.* But maybe he had wanted a more convenient place to dispose of the body, so he didn't have to drag her off, as he had the man in the tent. *If* he was the one who had killed the man and later removed the body—could it be true?

Yet how would she ever find the airfield without his help? She'd end up going in circles again, like yesterday. The sound of whistling coming from the camp's edge alerted her to Brad's return.

And here she stood, his knapsack open in front of her, caught red-handed.

What to do? She tried to refold the map, but it turned into an awkward wad of paper in her nerveless fingers. The next time he looked into his pack, he'd know at once that she had been prying. Too late. He lifted the tent flap as she fought with the sheet.

His expression altered when he saw her. He set down the black nylon backpack he carried, his blue eyes icy again. "Do you always go through other people's things?"

"Only when I doubt their motives," she retorted. "Why do you have this map? Did you kill the man in the tent?"

Brad grimaced. "Just because you think you saw—"

"I *did* see a dead man!" Ana interrupted. "And this map came from the table in my father's tent."

"Yes, it did," he agreed, his tone calm. "I saw it when I went in to investigate your tall tale. I took it because I wanted to check something out."

"You have no right to that map. It doesn't belong to you."

"Your father has no right to be pillaging the rain forest," Brad countered.

"He's not," Ana argued. "I know my father wouldn't do anything illegal."

66

Brad's handsome face scowled with derision. "Wake up. You can't be that naive. He has half the local officials on his payroll. No one's going to report him. And just because some of his company's actions are legal doesn't make them right." Quickly Brad reached for the map.

For a moment Ana stood rigid and unyielding. His accusations couldn't be true. Then, realizing the futility of a struggle, she released the sheet and watched him refold it and put it back in his pack.

"I don't believe you," she said finally. "And who are you to say? I don't know anything about you. You run around the jungle like an imitation Tarzan, pretending to be a native. . . ."

"I never said I was a native." He picked up the other backpack and handed it to her. "You can read my résumé later; we're wasting time. We have a long hike ahead of us. Here—I packed some supplies, and I'll show you how to roll up your hammock."

She felt the weight of the pack. "Whose supplies are these? And why is it so heavy?"

"I found them in another tent. Most of the weight comes from bottled water," he explained.

"Oh. But do I really need to carry so much water? We're only going back to the airfield." Despite the sting of his earlier accusations about her father, Ana realized with resignation that this arrogant stranger was still her only ticket to safety. As much as it galled her, she would have to try not to antagonize him too much. And there was simply no disputing the fact that he knew his way around the jungle, and she didn't. She was forced to rely on his judgment. But that didn't mean she couldn't ask questions.

"Listen, city girl, plans can change quickly in the jungle, and you won't find a drugstore or supermarket on every corner. If you want to stay alive, you do what I say. I'm leaving." Brad lifted the tent flap and strode out into the clearing.

"Wait!" She grabbed the knapsack and ran to her tent to collect her hammock. Then, loaded down with her flight bag and purse, and Brad's backpack over one shoulder, Ana followed him out of the clearing.

Within a few paces, they had plunged into the dim gloom of the rain forest. She glanced uneasily around her at the concealing trees. Was anyone else out here, waiting unseen behind a thick tree trunk? Better not to think about it. She had more prosaic concerns.

"Do you think we'll be able to stop for breakfast?" she asked mildly.

Brad's answer floated back through the heavy air. "I ate already. I was up an hour ago."

Annoyance made Ana's jaw tighten. *Thanks for telling me.* But she didn't say anything, and moments later he reached into his pack and handed her a granola bar. Ana took it grumpily, feeling more and more as though she were a novice skier on the bunny slopes in Vail. If only she were more prepared to deal with the jungle—if only she could be more self-sufficient. Then she could just stride off and leave *him* behind. Ripping the granola bar open, she stuffed the wrapping into her pocket and took a hungry bite. As she chewed, she cheered herself up by picturing her and Brad in a crowded metropolitan city: New York, or perhaps London or Rome. Confidently she gave a piercing whistle and a taxi screeched to a halt. She jumped in with an ease born of practice while Brad floundered on the sidewalk, whining for help. The daydream made her feel more cheerful.

A second later she tripped on a heavy root, and her daydream faded. She was still in this hateful jungle, her father was still missing, and she still had Brad's uncompromising back as her only companion. "Didn't you say that your mother lived in a camp near here?" Ana asked, determined to get more information out of him. "Where are you from originally? And what does she do out here?"

"Originally, Mom is from Akron, Ohio. She ended up here via the University of California at Los Angeles, Oxford University, and a lot of other places."

What kind of a nut was his mother, Ana thought, to come to this forsaken wilderness? She eyed Brad's ragged shorts, his dirty tennis shoes. Were they hiding out, in trouble with the law? How did he know so much about bribed government officials? Despite herself, she drew farther away from him. "Is she—"

"A drug smuggler?" Brad finished for her, his tone chilly. "Do you always think the worst of people? No, she's a scientist, a botanist. The rain forest has millions of plant species that are unique, often existing nowhere else on the planet. The native peoples have used local plants as medicines and foods for thousands of years, and the Western World knows nothing about them. One of the plants might be the cure for cancer, and we're destroying them before we even know what they are."

" 'We'?"

"Actually, 'you' would be more accurate," Brad told her, stepping around a large tree overhung with vines.

Ana shook her head, following in his steps. "Look, I just got here, and I'm leaving as fast as I can. I haven't done anything."

"You're Ana Puentes, right?" He made it sound like an accusation. "Puentes Industries has played its part in destroying the rain forest, cutting down and burning trees, strip-mining, killing the wildlife, turning the jungle into a wasteland."

"That's ridiculous!" Ana told him sharply. "My father would never do anything illegal."

"Who said it was illegal? Especially if you've bribed enough people to look the other way."

"You don't know what you're talking about," Ana said loftily. "Anyway, Brazil would probably be better off developing this wilderness. With all the hungry people in South America, this land could be growing grain instead of trees."

He stopped so suddenly that she walked into him. Hitting his backpack, she put out her hands and touched the tanned bare skin of his lower back. She felt taut muscles beneath her fingers before she stepped quickly away.

When Brad turned, his expression was fierce. "Listen, city girl, let me give you a five-minute lesson in the ecology of a rain forest."

Before she could protest, he knelt and dug through the thin layer of leaves. "See this?"

A large beetle scurried away, and Ana shivered involuntarily. She looked at the handful of dirt Brad had scraped up. It looked pale and sandy, without much substance.

"So?"

"This soil contains almost no minerals. It wouldn't support grain or even grass well."

"These trees look like they're doing all right." She waved at the immense trunks all around them, the leafy green canopy overhead.

"Do you know how plant life recycles itself in other climates?" he asked, with the careful patience usually reserved for a six-year-old.

"Yeah, sure," Ana retorted defensively. "The plants grow, die, and decay; the minerals go back to the soil; a new plant grows using those nutrients."

"Right. But in most of the rain forest, it rains so often that all the minerals are washed away. To survive, these plants hold the essential minerals within their own structures; the soil has almost nothing of value."

He allowed the sandy dirt to sift back between his fingers. "When these trees are cut down and burned, most of the nitrogen, sulfur, and carbon go up in smoke, and the remaining ash is washed away by the first rain. If you're lucky, you might harvest one crop. Then the rains cause erosion, and the earth bakes into useless hard clay. In two years the lush forest is dried-up wasteland."

"What about the natives? Don't they grow crops?"

"Some. But they clear few trees, and their small fields produce yields for only a season or two; then they move on. They do little harm to the ecological system, not like the big ranches southern Brazilians have tried to create, with little lasting success."

Despite herself, Ana was puzzled. "If that's true, why do settlers keep coming?"

"Hoping for a miracle, maybe, or just ignorant of the real nature of the land," Brad suggested. "The result is the same. But about fifteen percent of the earth's oxygen comes from the Amazon rain forest, from its plants' photosynthesis. If it's destroyed, the whole planet will suffer. Weather patterns could change from New York to Singapore."

Was this true? Ana shook her head, not sure whether to accept his words.

But Brad had concluded his lecture. Standing up again, he shifted his backpack and set out once more. She had to run to keep up with his long strides.

Before today, Ana would have said she was in good physical condition; she played tennis at school, rode horses, and swam. But within an hour, she was panting to keep up with Brad's seemingly effortless pace. She eyed his hard back and wide shoulders with dislike.

"Tarzan should get a load of you," she murmured.

"What?" Brad glanced back over his shoulder.

"You've got this routine down, don't you? Have you always lived in the Amazon?"

To her relief, Brad slowed his pace a little to answer. "Until recently, I spent most of my time back in the States. But my folks have been all around the world. All my summers and holidays I spend with my mom—in New Guinea or Africa, now here."

Brad's strides suddenly lengthened again, and she had to almost run to keep up, with no more breath for questions. Once he glanced back, and she thought she detected a glint of humor in his blue eyes. Did he enjoy making her scramble? Why did he hate the Puentes family so? Could his view of her father possibly be correct?

Ana struggled with the thought—still longing for the loving, regretful man who had written that last letter, the letter that had promised a new beginning for them. But what about the other, more familiar father, the father who was never there, always away on business, absorbed in corporate maneuvering?

Was it so hard to imagine that dedicated businessman sacrificing the environment to make a quick dollar? Ana shut her eyes briefly, praying that it wasn't her father who was raping the rain forest, hoping Brad could somehow be wrong.

And after all, she'd heard only Brad's opinion, Ana told herself. It was too soon to judge. Not to mention the fact that she couldn't care less about him. Just this morning she'd almost thought him a killer. Just because he had broad shoulders and a great body didn't mean his suspicions were accurate, didn't mean he was right about everything.

She followed him around yet another tree, then stopped abruptly as he paused. He stood very still; now what?

Already weary, though it was just midmorning, Ana grasped a vine on the nearest tree to lean on. Instantly a stinging pain shot through her palm. Jerking her hand back, she saw the long thorns she hadn't noticed on the hanging vines.

"Ouch!"

"Quiet," Brad whispered.

"The stupid vine attacked me," Ana explained, examining her bleeding hand.

"It's a liana, and it's not a vine. Actually it's a kind of tree," Brad told her softly.

"That figures." Ana rubbed her stinging palm. "I feel like Alice in Wonderland—nothing here is normal."

"Quiet," Brad repeated. "Do you hear that?"

Ana held her breath, wiping perspiration off her forehead. All her earlier fears rushed back. Were murdering natives following their footsteps? Why hadn't she listened to Raoul and stayed in Rio? Wistfully, she pictured herself sitting in an air-conditioned restaurant with a lavish menu to choose from, and a good-looking man across from her who didn't throw her granola bars or tell her to shut up.

"There!"

Ana listened hard and caught the faint sibilant hiss. Her skin rippled with goose bumps. "Is it a snake?" she whispered, stepping closer to Brad.

He shook his head, pointing.

She saw the ribbon of movement on the forest floor and held her breath. But instead of the giant snake she had feared, it was a line of dark dots.

Taking a step closer to look, she finally made out the column. "It's only ants," she said in relief.

Brad grabbed her arm, pulling her back. "Only ants? Those are army ants. They're a lot deadlier than an anaconda and can kill you a lot quicker."

Ana swallowed but didn't protest when he steered them carefully around the column of insects, which marched with almost mechanical precision across the forest floor, emitting a faint hiss.

When they had left the ants behind, he stopped unexpectedly and pulled a first-aid kit out of his backpack. "Let me see your hand."

Ana folded her arms instead. "It's not that bad." Being continually rescued by Brad was really starting to get on her nerves.

Brad rolled his eyes. "It's bleeding, isn't it? Some insects here are attracted to open wounds. They lay eggs under the skin. When the eggs hatch—"

Ana shuddered, a memory of the dead man in the tent flashing into her mind. Wordlessly she extended her palm and allowed him to clean the bloody punctures left by the large thorns, then wrap a gauze bandage around her hand. His touch was surprisingly gentle, and she stared at his dark head as he worked. Brad was impossible to predict. He held her wrist to steady her arm, and Ana wondered if her pulse had quickened, and if he could feel it. She felt her cheeks flush, very aware of the warmth of his fingers on her skin.

As if to confirm her thought, before he shouldered his backpack again, he took out a clean bandanna and offered it to Ana.

Her forehead was sticky with perspiration; the air under the trees was horribly hot and damp and still. After a moment's hesitation, she accepted the faded piece of cloth and wrapped it around her head, tying it firmly to keep her shoulder-length hair out of her face and prevent sweat from stinging her eyes.

"Thanks," she murmured.

"Just be careful what you touch next time, city girl," Brad advised. "That soft skin is too pretty to be used as a pin cushion."

His blue eyes crinkled. Ana wanted to smile back, but she wouldn't reveal the attraction she felt against all her better judgment.

"Tease me about being a city girl all you want—right now being in a city sounds like heaven. This place is impossible—there are dangers when you least expect them, and nothing is what you think it is."

Brad glanced at her. "And you're telling me that New York City is a safe place to live?"

"It's better than this," Ana said firmly. "As you pointed out, New York does have supermarkets and drugstores. Not to mention bathtubs and restaurants and taxis and—"

"There are hundreds of herbs and plants all around you that would make any drugstore look barren by comparison. All the other stuff you mentioned is just useless."

"I guess you prefer army ants and snakes and headhunters," Ana said. "You can't walk through the forest without running into danger at every step."

"Well, let's take the New York subway at midnight and see how long it takes us to be mugged." Brad grinned at her. "Or we could cross a Manhattan street at rush hour. Maybe even live to tell about it."

Ana laughed despite herself. "I take it you've been to New York?"

Brad nodded. "Not my favorite place."

"And this is?" Ana looked up at the thick canopy of green overhead, the towering tree trunks hung with lianas and other vinelike plants. "Early explorers called this the green hell, didn't they?"

"Or paradise," Brad countered, his blue eyes almost friendly. "It's all in the point of view."

"Maybe," Ana murmured. Brad stepped up his pace again, and she hurried to keep up. "Are we in a race?"

"I am," Brad told her. "I've got an urgent appointment to keep. I told you."

Sick children, he had said. Somehow she hadn't taken him seriously. Still, when they reached the airfield, both their problems would be solved. She could take her plane out of this jungle, get help to find her father, and Brad could fly to the native village and dispense whatever aid he was bringing. They must be getting close to the field—they'd been walking most of the morning.

Brad seemed to have the same thought. "Not far, now," he told her, looking almost sympathetic as she put one hand on her side, which was aching from their fast pace.

Pulling a plastic bottle out of her pack, Ana nodded, then gulped down some water. She had no breath left to talk. But she thought she saw more light ahead. Was the forest thinning? She sped up.

Yes, she could make out a clearing and the tumbledown building that was the airfield's only shelter.

The dirt field itself was bumpy and bare.

Bare.

Her chartered plane was nowhere in sight.

Seven

The plane couldn't be gone! She'd specifically told the crew to wait for her, no matter how long. Their fees had been guaranteed with her American Express card; the men couldn't have doubted that she'd pay them.

What else could go wrong? Ana felt almost light-headed with shock and fear. Now what would she do?

Beside her, she heard Brad say, "I thought you had a plane here."

"I did!" She spoke more sharply than she'd intended, but she felt overwhelmed by catastrophes. *Don't panic,* she told herself.

"Maybe the crew took it somewhere nearby to refuel," she said aloud, as much to herself as to Brad. "I didn't tell them exactly what time I'd return. Maybe they'll be back soon."

"Doesn't the airfield keep fuel here?" Brad pointed out. "What kind of operation does your father run?"

"I wish you'd stop attacking my father! He doesn't handle everything himself, you know." Ana glared at Brad.

Brad shrugged. "He is head of the company."

This was useless. She turned toward the building. "If the plane isn't close by, I'll radio for another."

"And a chopper for me, remember?" Brad lifted his brows as if she'd forgotten her promise already.

"Of course. I told you I always keep my word. My father taught me that." Her head high, Ana walked quickly toward the run-down building, and Brad followed her.

"*Olá!*" she called in greeting. When no one answered, she pushed open the door and walked inside.

She glanced at the desk almost fearfully, suddenly afraid of finding another prone body. But the chair behind the desk was empty. Where was the sullen man in the dirty uniform she had seen earlier, the one who had sent her down the river with the disappearing boat guide?

"There's no one here," Brad said.

"You have a gift for the obvious," Ana

snapped. "He has to be here somewhere." She opened an inner door and glanced into a back room. It appeared to be living quarters; she saw a hammock strung up from hooks and a pile of dirty laundry in the corner. But no sign of the missing man. Boxes stood against one wall, and Ana looked inside them. They held bottles of water and canned and dried food. Supplies for an extended stay; so why had he left?

Did he fear her anger over the boat guide who had abandoned her? But the airfield chief couldn't just disappear into the jungle, could he? Had he left with the missing plane? Why? And why had the plane departed, against all her orders? She felt less hope that the airplane would soon reappear, buzzing over the jungle to land again on the rough little field. But a plane was her only way out. Panic threatened again; she pushed it back and returned to the main room.

"Do you know how to work a radio?" she asked, looking over at Brad.

He had already crossed the room to stand in front of the row of electronic equipment. "Not this one."

"Why not?" Ana walked nearer to stare at the stacked units. "Oh!" Even she could tell that the ripped wires and shattered glass were not the radio's normal state. She swallowed hard. "This is impossible—not the radio, too. Who did this? And why?"

For a moment, she wondered wildly if Brad had broken the radio while she had been in the other room. But she would have heard the sound of breaking glass.

Brad frowned back at her. "No plane, and now there's no radio."

"Oh, Brad." Ana turned to him with wide eyes, very conscious of the fact that she had delayed him by almost a whole day to help her. But this wasn't her fault—she hadn't been lying about the plane. And she was stuck here too—it wasn't just he who was stranded.

"Sick children may die because I wasted time, against my better judgment, bringing you back here," Brad said angrily, reading her mind. "And now the chopper you promised me is a day-dream. I can't believe this. Why did I even listen to you?"

"It's not my fault," Ana argued, close to tears. "I'm as desperate for a plane or helicopter as you are. Oh, I wish I'd brought my cellular phone! But Mom said it wouldn't work in Brazil."

Surprisingly, Brad laughed. "Not many na-tives in the Amazon carry cellular phones, city girl." He turned aside to check one of the boxes by the wall and added several bottles of water to his knapsack, then shouldered it again.

"You can't be leaving?" Ana cried.

"Your memory's awfully short. I told you, I've wasted enough time. I've still got medicine to deliver."

"But you can't leave me here—what if the killers find me? We don't even know what happened to the airfield chief." Ana felt her stomach churn at the thought of being left in this deserted hut.

"If you avoid the lianas, you should be fine." Brad arched his dark brows till they almost touched the bandanna tied around his forehead. "Stay out of the jungle, and don't get sunstroke. There are plenty of supplies here; I'll check on you on my way back. If no one has returned by then, I'll take you to my mother's camp."

Ana opened her mouth, ready to plead with him to stay, then with great effort shut it. She wouldn't beg. His mind was obviously made up, and she'd just look stupid again. And did she really want to follow him back into the jungle? That thought was almost as frightening as remaining here. Inside the darkness of the rain forest lay insects and snakes and unknown natives; here she faced a smashed radio, a missing employee, and more unanswered questions.

Answers seemed to evade her in the jungle as well as out. This dash to the Amazon had been futile—more than futile: stupid and foolhardy. She was sore and tired and scared, and she had no idea where her father was, if he was dead or alive. Ana felt tears prickle behind her lids, but she refused to cry in front of Brad.

Instead she raised her chin and tried to make her tone as matter-of-fact as Brad's. "Sure, okay. I'll be fine."

"Sure you will," he agreed absently.

She wanted to yell at him, but she bit her lip. Watching him walk out of the hut and toward the jungle, she hugged herself, trying to contain her fright. But tears rolled down her cheeks, and she couldn't help sobbing aloud. She wept for her missing father and for herself, for the confusion she felt, for her uncertain situation. Why hadn't she called her mother at the airport? She'd be so worried by now.

I should have listened to Raoul, Ana thought, hunting for a tissue in her purse to wipe her damp face. But how could she give up her search for her father now? He had to be in trouble somehow—the signs seemed clear: the abandoned camp, the dead man, now the smashed radio. It all added up to some kind of horrible danger. And she and her father were in the middle of it.

Wearily Ana sat on the metal folding chair behind the beat-up desk. She thought wistfully of the sidewalk café in Rio where she had pictured them having a leisurely lunch. Afterward they could have strolled along the beach, talking. Was her father thinking of her, wherever he was?

Think positive. What if her imagination was simply running away with her? Maybe Brad was right. Maybe her father was off on another important business deal and had palmed her off on employees who had fallen down on the job. And yet, he had sounded genuinely pleased on the phone when she had accepted his invitation to visit. He'd promised to be at the airport.

"Oh, Dad," Ana muttered. "What's going on?"

Had Brad also been right about her father's activities in the rain forest? Ana pushed the thought away, not ready to face even more unpleasant conclusions.

This was useless. Ana blew her nose, then looked around for a rest room. Finally she located the latrine in back of the building. Coming back from the rough facility, Ana could almost feel eyes boring into her back.

"You're being silly," she told herself. But she walked more rapidly till she reached the shelter of the ramshackle building. Inside, she thought of the long hours, maybe days, that stretched ahead until Brad returned.

To divert herself, she examined the supplies in

the boxes and restocked her backpack with water bottles. Brad had said to be prepared, hadn't he? Anyhow, it gave her something to do.

She also went through her flight bag and took out her motion-sickness pills and the change of clothes. Later she'd figure out how to manage a sponge bath. The music tapes and makeup in her bag seemed like excess weight right now. She would leave them behind. There would be no problem replacing them when she got back to the city.

She stuffed her purse, along with her passport, travelers checks, credit cards and a little cash, and the pills Brad had given her, into her backpack, then took her malaria pills with a drink of bottled water. Soon she would inspect the cans of food in the boxes to see what her choices for dinner would be. First, though, she stopped at the desk, looking over the papers scattered across the top.

At least this time she saw no signs of dried blood. The writing was in Portuguese, of course, and Ana tried to pull up old memories to decipher the words. One sheet, heavy with figures, had a scrawled notation in the corner. That word—had she seen it on the map in her father's camp, the map that Brad had taken? She wrinkled her brow, trying to remember what it meant, when a sudden creak made her freeze, still bent over the desk.

It was the sound of the door opening. Fear held her motionless until a new thought brought a wave of relief. Brad must have come back for her.

She turned eagerly, then caught her breath in a gulp of dismay.

Two strangers stood between her and the outside door. Neither was a reassuring sight. The first man was big and burly, with dark hair straggling around his ears and a blue tattoo of a snake poised to strike showing on his bare arm. Ana's eyes widened as she made out the machete thrust into the thick belt he wore to hold up his worn denim jeans.

The second man was smaller, short and stout, wearing shorts and a T-shirt so grimy that the lettering was lost amid the stains. He had a limp mustache, and his expression was just as grim as his partner's.

"Who are you?" Ana asked, trying not to sound as terrified as she felt. "I'm looking for Jose Puentes. Do you work for him?"

The larger man frowned.

She had spoken in English, Ana realized. She repeated her question in Portuguese.

The big man grunted. "You, you answer us. Who sent you here?"

Ana blinked, bewildered by the hostile tone. "What do you mean?"

"Who sent you? You work for the government, or for that devil Manuel? He wants to stick his nose in our business, eh? You tell me, or I carve it out of you."

He pulled out the machete and gestured threateningly with it as he spoke.

Ana felt cold all over; she had to struggle to speak. "I don't know what you're talking about. I don't know any Manuel. I'm looking for my father, Jose Puentes. Do you know where he is?"

Blue Tattoo lowered his blade, and Ana could breathe a little easier. The two men spoke rapidly and softly to each other. Ana couldn't make out what they said. But when the bigger man turned back, she didn't like the look on his face.

He stretched his lips, but his grin was, if possible, even more frightening than his frown. "You don't know Manuel?"

"No, I swear it," Ana said quickly. "Just tell me about my father."

"Maybe. You be nice to us, maybe we tell you what you want to know."

He stepped closer, and she smelled rank sweat and a long-unwashed body. Ana felt her stomach churn. Backing away, she almost stumbled over her backpack. "Don't touch me!" she said sharply.

She picked up the pack, holding it in front of her like a shield.

But Blue Tattoo came closer. "You be nice to us, maybe we won't hurt you," he said this time.

Never had Ana felt such terror; it slowed her body—she felt as if she were barely moving. She wanted to run but knew she would never escape them. Even her brain didn't seem to be working properly. And Blue Tattoo was still between her and the door.

"I have money," she said quickly, trying to divert him. "I'll give it to you, if you leave me alone."

"American dollars?" His expression changed, his leer replaced by calculation. "Where?"

"There, in my bag," she told him. The expensive-looking flight bag sat against the wall where she'd abandoned it. Blue Tattoo turned, but his partner had already reached the bag, pulling at the zipper so impatiently that it snagged.

"Give it to me," Blue Tattoo warned, and the two men wrestled over the bag. Before they had time to discover that their booty consisted only of pricey cosmetics, Ana darted past them, snatching up the heavy backpack as she slipped out the door.

But as she moved, the big man looked up, growling like an animal. "You, stop!"

Ana ran for her life, letting the hut's ragged

screen door slam behind her. The outside air gave her hope. She ran across the clearing, praying she could make it into the trees where she might find a hiding place.

But almost instantly she heard the heavy lope of the two men behind her, and the big one shouted threats.

"I cut off your feet, little rabbit. Then where you run to?"

Gasping, Ana ran harder. In her flight, she stumbled over a submerged root, regained her balance with an effort, then ran on. The two men were closing the gap. She'd never make the concealing trees. But she wouldn't give up.

Almost there, Ana thought, *almost there*. Then a brutal hand gripped her arm, jerking her to a stop.

"No!" Ana had been clinging to the heavy backpack almost instinctively; now she tossed it at her attacker, but the big man shrugged it aside. His grip on her arm didn't loosen.

She swung at him wildly, but he laughed at the blow, then hit her hard across the face with his hand.

Her head snapped back, and Ana's eyes flooded with involuntary tears. Gulping back a sob, she put her hand to her bruised face as he pulled her toward the building. The other man watched them, grinning, and also turned back.

Jerked along by Blue Tattoo's rough grip, Ana had a hard time staying on her feet. But no doubt collapsing in the dirt would just make Blue Tattoo angrier.

And when they reached the hut again, he might—

Terror made her desperate. Just now he was looking away from her, taking her acquiescence for granted. Acting on a sudden impulse, she leaned down, biting hard into the hand that held her upper arm. She tasted salty blood, and he roared in pain.

His grip loosened for an instant, and Ana pulled away and ran once more for the trees.

One thing was certain: she couldn't let him catch her again. He lumbered after her with surprising speed, and his shouts held fierce anger. Ana gasped for breath, wishing desperately that she had never come to this savage green hell, where the humans were even more dangerous than the animals. She wished she were home again in New York, wished she were anywhere but here.

Feeling his breath on her back, she sensed that he was about to reach out to grab her. She jerked away, running awkwardly now like a wounded animal, her side aching, her lungs gasping for air.

It was hopeless. He was too close. Even though the trees were around them now, she'd never get far enough away to escape the man's sight. Ana wanted to sob, but she had no breath. Then she looked up and saw, as if out of nowhere, a bronzed native holding a bow, his long arrow cocked and ready, pointing straight at her.

Shocked at this new danger, Ana felt her knees weaken. She stepped into a slight depression in the forest floor, lost her footing, and tumbled to the ground.

She was close enough to detect the tiny movement of the native's arm. His arrow whistled through the air.

Eight

Bracing herself for the impact of the arrow, Ana cowered and covered her head with her hands. But the arrow flashed over her head, a speeding blur impossible to see.

Crashing through the growth behind her, Blue Tattoo yelled, a shout heavy with pain and outrage. Ana looked back and saw the arrow protruding from his chest. His eyes wide with shock, the big man toppled, like a tree falling. Behind him, his partner had done an abrupt about-face and had already retreated across a good part of the dirt field.

Now what? Her Brazilian adventure had been pushed to an even more unbelievable turn of events. No one back home would ever believe her tale. That is, if she ever got a chance to tell it. Ana pushed herself up to her hands and knees, watching the native warily. He wore only a brief loincloth and held his bow neatly to the side. It was taller than he. Ana wondered almost disinterestedly if she would be the next victim. If she was, there wasn't a lot she would be able to do about it, she realized. But the native stared at her, his brown eyes almost puzzled, then said something that Ana couldn't decipher.

Not another dialect—Ana smothered a groan. She shook her head and rose cautiously to her feet.

The native pointed to her head.

Was he a headhunter? Ana felt a stab of fear. Then she realized the bowman was pointing at the bandanna she wore tied around her forehead. He spoke again, and she heard the word *Brad*.

He knew Brad! He had recognized the faded bandanna that Brad had given her.

"Yes, I know Brad. I'm a friend of Brad's," Ana agreed, stretching the truth a bit as she pointed to the bandanna she wore. Fervently she hoped this was the right response.

"Brad," the bowman repeated, and added a few more words she didn't understand.

"You know where to find Brad?" Ana asked. She pantomimed again. "You take me to Brad?"

The native stared at her, his expression hard

to read. Did he understand? Would he help?

Behind her was at least one thug, maybe more. Ahead of her was a deadly jungle maze. *Please,* she thought.

The native seemed to make a decision; he turned and headed back into the trees. He was leaving her! But then he looked over his shoulder, giving her a slight wave. The gesture was unmistakable.

"Yes," Ana said. "I'm coming." She ran, circling the body of the tattooed man, retrieved the backpack she had thrown at him, then hurried back. To her relief, the native waited, looking at her supplies almost with amusement, then set out through the trees. He went at a steady lope, and Ana hurried to keep up, just as she had with Brad.

They walked until darkness fell, supplanting the eternal forest gloom with true night. The air, so hot and muggy when they'd started, had cooled until Ana shivered.

She was tired and out of breath, but she didn't dare fall behind; she'd never find her way out of this jungle alone. She had thought Brad was hard to follow, but at least she could talk to him, ask for a short break. With the native, she could only struggle along, her sides aching and her legs sore from the unaccustomed hiking. Her shoulders felt as if the straps of her backpack were permanently engraved in them, and her feet were killing her, rubbed raw and bleeding from broken blisters.

How could he see where he was going? Twice Ana barely avoided walking into a tree, and she could barely make out the shape of her guide, only a few feet ahead of her.

Glancing ahead, she thought she saw a glimmer of light; then it was gone. Ana sighed in disappointment. No, there it was again, winking at her. Trees hid the tiny flame momentarily as they moved forward; then it appeared again.

It was a minute campfire, with a simple shelter set up behind it in the small clearing. Brad jumped to his feet as they materialized out of the darkness. She could have hugged him—he looked suddenly like an old and dear friend. For an instant she forgot all their earlier antagonism.

"What are you doing here?" His dark brows were arched again; she hated that look.

Feeling thankful that she hadn't voiced her first elation, she said, "I decided to come with you."

"You can't," he said flatly. "It isn't safe."

Ana laughed wildly. "Safe? That word has little meaning in this part of the world."

"Look," he said, with an obvious attempt at patience, "you don't know what you're getting into."

"And you don't know what I'm getting out of," she retorted.

Brad looked genuinely puzzled. "What are you talking about?"

"Ask your friend," Ana said. Brad hadn't believed her about the body in the tent; why would he believe her now about the attack by the tattooed man?

But when she looked around for confirmation of her narrow escape, the native had gone, melting into the forest like a wisp of fog. "Damn. Does he do that a lot?"

Brad shook his head. "Arabu has his reasons. Looks like I'm stuck with you."

"Thank you for the overwhelming welcome." Ana sat down on the bare ground in front of the tiny fire. Her relief at seeing a familiar face had revived her for a moment, but now exhaustion threatened to overwhelm her. She pulled a water bottle from her backpack and took a long drink.

"Are you hungry?" Brad asked, sounding almost concerned.

Although she hadn't eaten anything since that morning, Ana shook her head. "I'm too tired to eat. Save your granola bars."

He grinned reluctantly. "Give me your hammock; I'll show you how to string it up."

The little shelter was going to be cramped quarters, but she could hardly complain, Ana thought as she watched Brad hang her hammock next to his. The poles were slim but sturdy. This time, Ana made no question about the strange sleeping arrangements. She didn't try to undress, just unrolled her blanket and wrapped it around her, then climbed into her hammock while Brad went back outside to make sure the fire was out.

In the more intense darkness, she heard him slip into his own hammock, then felt the poles sway as Brad's weight was added to her own. The two string hammocks were so close together that she could feel his hip brush her own, and his arm rubbed her shoulder as he settled himself. It was hard to relax with Brad so close to her in the blackness.

Tired as she was, Ana found sleep eluding her. She listened to the sounds of the jungle after dark. A sound like a rusty swing made her start; then she realized it must be some kind of birdcall. Whistles and croaks and sometimes shrill shrieks filtered through the darkness. Even lying in the hammock, she felt stiff, unable to relax, too aware of unseen creatures roaming the wilderness, and no walls to shut them out.

"Don't worry—nothing's going to get you," Brad said quietly through the thick darkness.

Ana blinked; she'd thought he was asleep. "How do you know so much?" she asked. "Just from your summers spent with your parents?"

"Uh-huh. My dad taught me to tread lightly, to bury my fires, to respect the world around me."

He'd said his mother was American. "Is your father American also?"

"English," he told her easily. "He was from the Cotswolds. Beautiful land. But during my childhood we lived all around the world."

"Really?" Ana turned her head, surprised to find that she and Brad actually had something in common, then lay still again as the hammock swayed beneath her. "My father's Brazilian, and my mother's American. Do you ever wonder just where you belong?"

He chuckled softly. "Afraid you don't fit in, you mean? I see it more as an opportunity—you can make yourself whatever you wish to be. I don't want to be typecast."

An opportunity, this brash young adventurer said. Brad was unique, that was true enough. What about Ana—who did she choose to be? She sighed, then felt the warmth of Brad's fingers as he reached out to touch her cheek lightly. "You'll be okay, city girl."

Brad could be so rude, and then so understanding. What if her father was a criminal, as

Brad had suggested—what did that make her? If she'd known her father better, if he'd spent more time at home when she was younger, Ana thought with her old anger, she wouldn't be so confused right now.

She pulled her blanket more tightly around her; the air was cool against her cheek. Brad didn't speak again, and soon she heard his breathing, regular and unhurried. He was asleep. She was conscious of how close Brad was; his nearness was both disturbing and reassuring. The warmth of his body slowly reached out to engulf her, and Ana felt her tension fade. She heard one last shriek and thought in a muddled way, *They should feed those monkeys*. Then she slept.

When she woke, the first rays of sunlight were just lightening the darkness, but already the other hammock hung limp and empty. Trying to roll smoothly out of her own string bed, Ana fell in a heap to the ground. Grateful that Brad hadn't seen, she scrambled up and rubbed her feet and legs, which felt numb from her cramped sleeping position. Ana folded her blanket, found her backpack, and took a small mirror from the outside pocket.

Her face looked gray and mottled in the dim light, and below her left eye was an ugly eggplant-colored bruise from where Blue Tattoo had hit her. Ana grimaced. There was nothing she could do about it. She combed some of the snarls from her hair, then braided it to keep it out of her face. Brad's faded bandanna was re-wrapped around her forehead. Just as she was wishing for a chance to use her toothbrush, Brad came back into sight.

"Come and eat; then we're pulling out."

At least he hadn't eaten without her, she realized, feeling more cheerful than she had since she'd arrived in Brazil. Ana went eagerly toward the smell of hot food, suddenly reminded of the yawning empty spot inside her. Brad had heated a mixture of dried vegetables and rice over his small fire. It was a strange breakfast, but Ana ate quickly, bent over her tin plate. When she rose and went to help Brad clear up, he looked at her in surprise.

"What happened to your face?"

Ana touched her sore cheek gingerly. "I got hit."

"By who?" Brad demanded, frowning. He held her chin and examined the bruise more closely.

Ana felt a flicker of pleasure, whether from Brad's touch or the anger she saw in his face, she wasn't sure. "I didn't stay around long enough to find out his name. Two men came to the airfield hut. They thought I knew someone called Manuel. Do you know who that is?"

Brad shook his head. "Maybe one of the local smugglers. Why did he hit you?"

Shrugging, Ana said, "They threatened to hurt me—one of them had a machete. When I broke away from them and ran, he caught me and hit me. He was dragging me back to the hut when I bit him, and then I ran."

Blue eyes looked into hers. "You bit him?"

Ana nodded. "Yeah. Then right as he was about to catch me again, your friend with the bow shot him."

Brad nodded slowly, as if murder in the jungle were an everyday occurrence. Maybe it was. Again Ana wished she were back in the city; at least she understood urban crime, knew a little about how to avoid it. Natives with arrows were beyond her.

Brad stepped away; he seemed to consider the subject closed. He opened his backpack and inspected a padded square bag with a zipped top.

"What's that?" Ana asked.

He glanced at her. "Mom and I rigged up a chemical cold pack to keep the medicines cool, but I'm not sure how much longer it will last."

And she had delayed him. Ana felt a flicker of guilt, which she tried to assuage by helping as he efficiently and rapidly broke camp. They buried the garbage and the ashes of the fire, then once more set out into the green gloom of the tall trees.

Brad set a rapid pace, but at least there was no more talk of leaving her behind. Ana thought ruefully that she owed Blue Tattoo for that, at least, and for finally convincing Brad that some of her fears were real.

But Brad's concern seemed short-lived; the rest of the day he paid little heed to her, and Ana labored to keep up with him. They took occasional short breaks to drink from their water bottles or chew on a food bar, but the rests were never long enough.

The trees seemed to revolve around them, and Ana felt as if they were on a carousel. She had the crazy notion that they were getting nowhere.

"Are you sure you know where you're going?" she asked him finally, when they had been walking for several hours.

Brad nodded, pausing to take a swig of water and wipe his forehead. "The river's just ahead." He pointed.

"The river?" Ana tried to see through the trees.

"I left a canoe there a few weeks ago. If we're lucky, it will still be there. Then we can go by water the rest of the way."

"Thank goodness," Ana murmured, thinking with relief of the chance to sit down. Then she remembered all the perils in the local rivers and wondered if the new form of travel would really be an improvement. "Are there rapids?"

"Nothing worth mentioning," Brad said offhandedly.

She frowned at him. "Look, I've risked my life enough on this trip. We don't have to go out of our way to court disaster. You're not one of those macho guys who thinks it's fun to go white-water rafting, or anything, are you?"

"Thank you for the instant character analysis, city girl," Brad retorted dryly. "No one asked you to come along, remember?"

"I didn't have much choice," Ana couldn't help pointing out. Her temper was short, after the long morning's trek. She was tired, hot, and dirty, and it was hard to stay calm. "Stay there and be murdered, come with you and drown. All I want to do is find my father and get out of this horrible place. I hate the jungle!" She turned and gave a resounding slap to the closest tree.

Immediately, dark dots dropped out of the tall branches, hitting her shirt with tiny plops. Ana shook her head and felt a sudden prick, then searing pain on her back and arms.

"Help!" She slapped at her back. "Oh!"

"Looks like fire ants," Brad said helpfully. "Take off your clothes and shake them out."

Pausing only long enough to give him a panicked glare, Ana ran through the trees, driven by continuing stabs of pain. Where was the river Brad had promised? There, just ahead, she saw the glint of water.

Gasping, Ana dropped her backpack and rushed into the water. She pulled off her top and shorts and threw water over her torso. A couple of ants slipped away in the water—such small things to hurt so much. Her body still ached, but the stabbing agony was slowly fading.

"Thank heavens," Ana muttered, weak with pain. The water, though not cool, felt wonderful against her hot, sweaty skin. Then she took a closer look and felt a shock of surprise. The river looked almost red! Was it blood?

Ana straightened, then leaned back to examine the darkish water. Dipping her hands into the strange liquid, she stared at the red-black water in her palms. It looked almost like cola.

But it still felt refreshing after her hot hike and the stinging ant bites. She walked farther into the river, bending to let it wash over her, splashing her face.

Brad emerged from the trees. To her embarrassment, he seemed to be laughing. "You okay?"

"Yeah," she muttered. "Unless they were deadly poisonous ants or something." A sudden thought rocked her, and she examined several of the angry-looking red bites. "Were they?" she asked suspiciously.

Trying to smother his grin, Brad shook his head no. "Not this time. But in the future you may want to think twice before attacking a tree. The jungle fights back, as you've discovered." He walked to the bank and dropped his pack.

"You could have told me," she muttered, suddenly conscious that she was wearing only her wet bra and panties. She looked around to retrieve her clothes, grabbing her top as it floated away, finding her sodden shorts snagged on a fallen tree limb. "What's wrong with the water?"

"Didn't you know that the rivers in the Amazon Basin have colors?" Brad waded cautiously into the river as he answered. "This is a black river."

"Why?"

"It has more runoffs, more minerals," he explained.

"It's so strange," Ana said, dipping her hand into the dark water in fascination. Her entire visit to the Amazon had been filled with one bizarre, unique discovery after another.

"It's all we have at the moment. And you did need a bath," Brad said cheerfully.

That was too much. Her eyes widened in indignation. "And you don't?" she demanded. Tossing her wet clothes to the bank, Ana cupped her hands and slapped the water, sending a small wave toward Brad. The liquid splashed him on the side of the face. He blinked in surprise, and Ana laughed.

"Think you're funny, huh?" He splashed back at her, and she ducked out of the way, giggling.

For a few moments, they battled furiously, then Brad called, "Ana! Don't back up any farther."

"Why not?" Ana asked, wary of a new trick.

"There's a caiman behind you." Brad's voice was calm.

Ana jumped. "A what?" Looking behind her, she saw the strip of brownish green that had been masked by a clump of grass. Now she saw the beady eyes and the narrow nostrils of the half-hidden reptile.

"Oh! An alligator!" Stepping quickly away from it, she wavered, almost slipping on the uneven river bottom. Instinctively she reached for Brad, throwing her arms around him for support.

Without hesitation, he held her close. "Caiman," he corrected gently. "Like an alligator."

Ana felt the reassuring strength in his body,

the firmness of his muscled torso and broad shoulders. His bare chest touched her wet skin. Ana's heart, which had raced when she saw the caiman, now beat quickly for a totally different reason.

What was she thinking? She wasn't even sure she trusted this self-assured hybrid who made his way so easily through the gloomy pathways of the rain forest.

Knowing that her cheeks were red, Ana dropped her hold and backed away. Yet she felt a pang when she stepped out of his arms.

"It's only a small caiman," Brad told her, his voice even. But she could swear there was a glimmer in his blue eyes that hadn't been there before. "At least there aren't any piranhas here."

"What?" Ana forgot everything and peered anxiously at the water. "Good grief. Nothing's safe around here."

"Go ahead and take a quick wash, if you want; I have soap in my pack. But don't strip completely, and don't go in too deep." He walked back to the bank, rummaged in his backpack, and tossed her a bar of camping soap.

"I wasn't planning on either one," Ana told him quickly, not quite meeting his eye.

Brad grinned wolfishly. "No, I mean, there are other dangers besides piranhas. A little fish called the candiru likes to lodge itself in a person's . . . well, orifices. It has barbs and has to be cut out."

Ana shuddered at the thought. "What other wonderful surprises does the river hold? Snakes?"

"Those, too. And electric eels, and giant catfish that will swallow half your leg. Just stay near the shore and keep your eyes open."

Ana needed no further urging. She washed quickly in the river, noting with satisfaction as the days-old grime dissolved from her arms and legs. Then she scrubbed her clothes, rubbing them with soap and wringing them out. Before putting them on, she checked carefully for ants, leeches, or any other unwanted guests. The garments felt damp and soggy, and in the humid air the sunlight would be slow to dry them. Ugh. Then she remembered the change of clothes in her backpack. With relief, Ana waded to shore and pulled on dry clothes; she couldn't do anything about her soggy sneakers.

Brad washed quickly also; she tried not to stare. The way her stomach quivered when she glanced at his tanned shoulders or well-muscled back was ridiculous. She wasn't interested in him—they barely got along! Ana tried to pull up memories of Barry, her ex-boyfriend. He'd been a polite senior with an impeccable family background and an enviable GPA. Next to Brad, he seemed as dull as chalk dust. Ana found that suddenly the thought of their breakup didn't produce even a glimmer of regret.

Brad shaved with a small razor, then pulled on clean shorts and wrung out his bandanna. Then he picked up his backpack again and made his way carefully along the riverbank, staring into the shallows.

"What are you looking for?" Ana called.

"There!"

Nine

"What is it?" Ana repeated, looking nervously around for a new enemy.

Openly relieved, Brad said, "My canoe—it's still here." He waded through the water and pulled the small vessel out from its hiding place. After clearing away the palm leaves that had protected it from rainwater, he checked it out carefully. "Looks in one piece, too. I thought the termites might have found it. Put your stuff in, and let's get going. We'll go a lot faster now."

Ana swung her backpack into the small craft, then climbed in gingerly, feeling it move beneath her. Kneeling on the rough-hewn wood, she accepted the oar that Brad passed up.

"Ever paddled a canoe?"

"Not since summer camp." Ana was annoyed

to hear Brad chuckle. "Why didn't you go by water all the way?" she asked quickly, not wanting to hear any more "rich city girl" cracks.

"Big rapids downstream," he told her. "But this part of the river is relatively calm."

At first, the river seemed to live up to Brad's assessment. Floating on the peaceful stream, dipping her oar into the dark liquid as she tried to match Brad's seemingly effortless rhythm, Ana felt more relaxed than she had in days.

The sky overhead was clear and a deep blue; the jungle crowding each bank looked deceptively serene. A large butterfly fluttered at the marshy river edge. Only an occasional bird or monkey call broke the midday silence, and even the plop of a caiman sliding into the water caused her only a moment of alarm. The reptile seemed to ignore their canoe, and Ana's strokes returned to their steady pattern.

But then they rounded a bend in the river, and she blinked in dismay. The smooth surface of the water now swirled with tumultuous currents. Arcs of white spray partially hid huge boulders jutting into the formerly placid flow of the river. Ana stopped paddling and stared at them in horror. Even without her help, the rapids were coming up all too fast.

"Avoid the rocks," Brad yelled unnecessarily

over the louder rush of the river.

No duh. Ana paddled with renewed urgency, working hard to aim their little canoe away from the biggest boulders. But though she managed, with Brad's help, to steer away from the first obstacle, an almost hidden jagged stone suddenly appeared just beneath the dark water, and she had to turn the boat again.

Her shoulder muscles strained as she pushed hard against the roiling water, forcing the canoe away from the sharp edge of the submerged rocks.

Time seemed to slow as she fought with the river; it was only Ana and her wooden paddle, straining against a force older and bigger and stronger than she. She forgot even Brad, paddling furiously behind her; it was her own personal fight against the river. When the canoe slid away from the menacing edges of stone, she felt a thrill of elation. "We did it!"

They slipped into calmer water again, and Ana could take a deep breath.

"Good going!" Brad called from behind her.

She looked over her shoulder to grin at him, sharing this victory.

"Not bad for a city girl," he said.

Feeling smug, Ana turned back to her paddling, rubbing one hand across her forehead.

Beads of perspiration mixed with spray from the river, and the bandanna she still wore was soaked, as well as her cotton T-shirt. But the wet cloth soon felt good as the sun's rays beat down upon them, and she paddled steadily as they made their way upriver.

When Brad pointed the canoe toward the bank, she felt relief, glad for a chance to stop and rest her arms. They came aground on a marshy piece of bank, and Brad jumped out. Ana followed, and they pulled the canoe out of the water. After they removed their packs, Brad hid the canoe again before they turned into the forest.

Ana drank from her water bottle, and Brad handed her a granola bar from his pack, which she accepted with a nod of thanks. The shared canoe journey, in which she had acquitted herself well for the first time, seemed to have softened their earlier mutual antagonism.

The jungle felt almost familiar when they plunged back into its green dimness. Steadily they walked through tall trees, a thick leafy ceiling overhead. Ana waited for her eyes to adjust to the gloom, then stared at the thick trunks draped with lianas, sometimes growing brightly colored mushrooms and other fungi. She remembered their earlier debate—was this place a primeval paradise, rich with natural treasures if you knew where to look, or the green hell that early explorers had called it, full of dangers and deadly surprises?

Perhaps both. Her knowledge of the place was growing. She felt almost like a seasoned traveler, treading the thin layer of dead leaves that covered the forest floor, keenly aware of her path, watching for ants, snakes, and other forest inhabitants.

Still, she didn't detect the wall of leaves and thatch rising out of the trees until they were almost upon it.

To her surprise, Brad put out one hand to stop her. "Ana, I haven't explained why this visit is so dangerous."

She gave him her full attention. "Is the tribe warlike?"

His answer did little to reassure her. "Not more than most," he told her. "It's what I have to do here."

"I thought you were bringing medicine to sick children."

He nodded.

"So? How can that be dangerous?" Ana frowned. Just as she was feeling more at home in the rain forest, new puzzles appeared.

"The tribes don't understand disease. Many of their illnesses have appeared along with the white strangers who come into the jungle from outside."

"White people brought in disease?" Ana felt

sudden sympathy; the same thing had happened to North American tribal peoples, too, centuries ago. Common European illnesses had proved fatal to thousands of Native Americans.

Brad nodded. "One photographer with the flu wiped out a whole village. Cold germs can kill these people, who've built up no immunity. We try to avoid tribes that haven't been contacted—it disrupts their own culture—but this tribe had already been approached by Westerners, hence the diseases. The thing is, natives here think that illness is the result of someone's bad wishes."

"Like a spell?" Ana suggested, remembering old superstitions.

Brad nodded. "And this has to be avenged. So if the medicine I bring helps these children, the tribe will thank me. But if the kids are too sick, if the antibiotics don't work, their parents could consider me—and you—murderers."

Ana felt cold. "If it's so dangerous, why did you come?"

"Because I know these people—they saved my life once. And the kids will die if nothing is done," Brad told her simply.

Ana sighed. "I don't really have any choice, do I? Let's go—we're wasting time."

Brad smiled at her, a real smile that almost

made up for the chill of fear inside her. "Come on, then."

They walked closer, and she saw that the structure was a huge circular building made of thatched leaves. A dog barked sharply from inside, and two naked youngsters, their brown eyes round with surprise, came out to gaze at them.

"This is a tribe of the Yanomami," Brad murmured. "The whole tribe lives together in the yano. Stay behind me for a moment."

Ana, not sure if this was native custom or protection from danger, nodded.

They entered the large shelter, and Brad paused, speaking in rapid-fire pace a highly stressed language Ana had never heard before.

Someone emerged from the group of people at the other end of the circular building; it was a woman.

She stared at Brad for an instant, then smiled and spoke rapidly in the same language.

Ana tried not to stare. The woman stood under five feet, and her smooth brown skin was streaked with wavy red markings. She wore a waistband decorated with red cotton fringes about three inches long, and nothing else. Her breasts drooped, and her straight dark hair was worn in a short bowllike cut. Two large green leaves were tucked through her pierced ears.

More women and older girls came closer to see the visitors. Ana felt like a giant, but she smiled at the women, who smiled back, apparently friendly enough. They wore similar brief costumes; many had their bodies decorated with patches of red paint in various designs.

They also wore armbands, sometimes with green leaves or bright bird feathers attached, and leaves or feathers were also tucked through their pierced ears. Ana stared at an older girl who wore a thin sliver of wood through her nose, with matching sticks of wood hanging from her lower lip.

Ana blinked. *Savage,* she thought. Then she remembered a girl at school who had gotten collagen injections to make her lips plumper, and her best friend, Valerie, with her triple-pierced ears. There were different kinds of savagery, she mused.

Brad was moving forward, so she followed him. When they stepped inside the shadow of the thatched roof, Ana saw that the yano was built in a doughnut shape, with the center part of the roof open to the sky.

Around the sides, each family had its own small fire, with the ever-present hammocks strung up in groups of three from the yano poles, and a hearth fire in the center of each triangle. Shelves against the wall held fruit and other foodstuffs, and clay pots and bows and arrows were stacked underneath.

"Where are the men?" Ana asked Brad in a whisper.

"Hunting, or working in the tribe's gardens."

Two elderly men were sitting by a fire, their backs to her. Both men and women wore their thick dark hair in the same circular cut. One woman sat on the hard-packed earth in front of a simple loom, a naked baby in her lap, her hands busy with her work.

"Weaving cloth?" Ana guessed, watching the length of fabric grow.

"A cotton hammock," Brad corrected. "In a warm, humid climate, clothes are mostly a nuisance. The Yanomami idea of clothing is pretty minimal."

That was the truth, Ana thought, looking around them. Then the first woman led them to a group of hammocks, where a child lay sluggish and still.

The woman spoke, and Brad interpreted for Ana. "She says the shaman has chanted and danced for three days, but the children have not improved."

Ana looked at the little girl. Her eyes were dull, her bronze skin mottled with a rash and flushed with fever. Not far away, a small boy moved rest-

121

lessly, whimpering. The women around them murmured with concern. Ana felt another stab of fear. Were the children too ill to be helped? Would she and Brad pay for the little ones' deaths with their own lives?

But it was too late to back out. Brad touched the little girl's forehead gently, then lifted her eyelid as the child coughed hoarsely.

"Do you know what's wrong?" Ana asked in a low tone.

"Measles, probably gone into pneumonia. I've seen a lot of it among the tribes," Brad answered. "Maleo says four children have already died; she lost an infant last week. I don't know which ones— she can't speak the names of the dead."

He crouched on the bare earth floor and took out the cold pack from his bag.

"Is the medicine still okay?" Ana asked.

"I think so."

Ana watched with new respect as he filled a syringe from a small vial.

"Can I help?"

"Wipe their skin," he told her, tossing her a box of alcohol wipes.

Clumsily she opened the foil wrapping and, at his direction, cleaned a spot on the little girl's skinny hip. The child's skin was hot under her hands. Ana watched as Brad carefully inserted the needle. The little girl cried out, but Ana held her hand and spoke softly, distracting her until the needle was withdrawn. Brad rubbed the sore spot, speaking to the toddler soothingly in her own tongue.

When he stepped away, the woman cradled her daughter, murmuring words of comfort. Ana could see the worry in the mother's dark eyes. Oh, if only this worked!

They repeated the performance with the other children; then Brad prepared other injections of measles vaccine for the tribe members who had not yet shown signs of the illness. "How about you? Had all your shots?" he asked Ana.

"Yes, before I left," Ana answered, not looking up from her task.

Later, when darkness neared, the men returned to the yano in small groups. Some bore the results of their labors, and the women and children came to see what they'd be having for dinner. Ana saw a basket filled with vegetables, assorted fish, and two large monkeys hanging limply from a pole.

"Monkey on the menu? Great. What I'd give for a pizza to go," Ana murmured to herself.

Brad was greeted by the headman; he talked to the hunters, and soon the men also received immunizations. While she listened to the sharp staccato chatter, Ana tried hard not to stare. The men wore thin cotton waistbands and occasional patches of paint. Period.

The year before, Ana had visited a French nudist beach with her mother, but this felt inexplicably different. All the same, she kept her gaze level and her expression calm. *It's perfectly natural with them,* she told herself sternly. *I will not stare; it's silly and rude.*

But she was glad when the last man had received his shot and Brad put away his syringes. Then he went back to check on the sick children, and she followed.

"How are they? Any improvement?"

Brad touched the little girl's cheek. "Still feverish. Too soon to tell, I guess. All we can do now is hope for the best."

Ana patted the child's arm, with a silent but fervent prayer for her recovery. Her mother had already lost one child; this little one, with her smooth copper skin and dark eyes flushed with illness—she couldn't die too.

"Get well, sweetie," Ana whispered.

And if not, she remembered their own peril. How quickly could these friendly people turn violent? Ana hoped she didn't have to find out.

Leaving the mothers sitting by the hammocks, Ana and Brad walked away from the children.

Ana saw a puppy limping across the open space of the yano, a smallish mongrel hobbling on swollen paws.

"Poor thing; what's wrong with him?" Ana asked Brad quietly.

"Burrowing fleas. Don't go barefoot, and remember your insect repellent."

Ana shivered, sure that was one precaution she wouldn't forget to take. Quietly they strung up their hammocks in the space the headman indicated and sat there, watching the women cook over the open fires. Ana saw that the smoke drifted up to the center opening of the yano and seemed to keep out most of the mosquitoes that roamed the night air. Some of the women baked manioc bread in thin flat cakes on a clay plate placed over the cooking fire; others prepared the fish and game that the hunters had brought in.

When the cooking was completed, Ana found that most of the adults lay back in their hammocks, totally at ease. From there, they reached into the cooking pot pushed to the side of each family's fire, spearing bites of food with small wooden sticks. Brad cheerfully did the same, but Ana felt her stomach quiver.

"Thanks, I don't think I'm very hungry," she said faintly.

"Trying to insult your hosts?" Brad asked, his tone cool.

Oh, great. Ana accepted a clean stick and poked it into a morsel of food, pretending to nibble.

"Tell the truth—it's not half-bad," Brad challenged, his blue eyes glinting with laughter.

"No, no, sautéed monkey has always been one of my favorites," Ana retorted.

"I guess you'd rather eat caviar and escargot," Brad said considerately. "After all, fish eggs and snails are *much* better than monkeys."

Narrowing her eyes, Ana swallowed hard and lowered her stick. She dropped the piece of meat into the dust, letting one of the dogs snap it up. "That's it; I'm full. Thank you very much."

Ignoring his snort of laughter, Ana lay back in her hammock. Tarzan here could enjoy the jungle cuisine. For herself, room service and a hot shower would be welcomed. And yes, she thought silently, she *would* prefer caviar and escargot. Any normal person would.

After the meal, there was a good deal of talk and laughter around the fires, which Ana listened to without comprehending. A young girl whose ears were adorned with scarlet parrot feathers smiled hopefully at a young man; their conversation, conducted with giggles, was easy enough to guess at.

But when another young man stared at her, Ana's amusement faded. He walked closer and spoke to her, but the words meant nothing. She sat up in her hammock, looking uneasily toward Brad for a translation.

Instead, Brad leaned closer, throwing one arm around Ana's shoulders, and spoke to the young native in a friendly tone. Ana blinked in surprise as Brad suddenly turned and kissed her—a long, lingering kiss. His lips were warm and firm, and part of Ana wanted to respond. But she was also aware of their interested audience, and she felt her cheeks flush when Brad pulled away. He spoke to the watching natives, and the Yanomami laughed. The young man nodded and walked on to another group.

Ana tensed, staring at Brad with her brows lifted. "What did you say to him?"

His arm still draped possessively around her shoulders, Brad grinned at her mockingly. "I told him you're my wife."

Ten

"What?" Ana heard the shrillness in her reply. "Why did you tell him we're married?"

"For your own protection," he told her casually. "I've been adopted as a 'brother-in-law' to the headman, Tomi. But a brother-in-law's sisters are prime marriage possibilities for Tomi's relatives, so you're better off as my wife than my sister. Or even friend."

"Oh," Ana said, trying to digest a new set of customs in one pithy nutshell. She should have bristled at his touch. Instead, she was surprised to find how much Brad's closeness affected her. She liked the comforting warmth of his body, the strength of his arms. It was almost too bad this was only pretense, she thought, wishing she could lean into his embrace. Then, regretting her momentary weakness, she drew back. "Just don't let it go to your head."

He dropped his arm quickly. "Not likely, city girl."

Ana frowned and pointedly looked the other way.

Later, as monkeys shrieked, birds chattered, and crickets hummed quietly, Ana felt very much alone in the dense tropical darkness. She'd never tell him so, but she felt secretly glad to have Brad's hammock so close to her own, glad that as the tribe lay sleeping around them, with a whole jungle just outside, she was close enough to reach out and touch his arm.

In the flickering glow of the dying fire, she stared at Brad's closed eyes, his lashes dark against his cheek, then looked across the yano to the portion of the shelter where the sick children lay. Would they pull through?

Ana found sleep hard to capture. But the crickets' chirps finally blended into a faraway chant, and she closed her eyes.

She woke to hear a dog barking, then a loud, emphatic flow of words from the headman. Afraid to open her eyes, Ana felt her whole body tense, sensing danger in the headman's formal pronouncements.

In a moment, the man's voice dropped away, and she heard an excited murmur of voices on the other side of the yano. Ana opened her eyes, blinking at the brightness of the tropical morning, then gasped. A tribesman stood beside her hammock, a deadly looking machete in his hand. He stared down at her.

Wildly, she looked past him for help, but Brad's hammock hung limp and empty. She should be used to it by now, she thought inconsequentially. But where was he? Had he been murdered already? Was she next?

Ana held her breath.

Then she saw that the native's grip on the machete was relaxed, and his expression was more curious than angry. She nodded to him, struggled up, managed to slip out of the string bed without falling. Looking across the yano, she saw Brad. He was alive!

Relief flooded through her. Was it only practical relief that her guide was safe and she wasn't stranded alone in the wilderness—or was it more?

Brad stood beside the campfire where one of the sick children had rested. A good portion of the tribe seemed to be gathered around them, and some of the voices were loud. Ana felt renewed anxiety.

She couldn't see Brad's face. Were the

Yanomami about to turn on them? Should she make a run for the jungle?

But she couldn't abandon Brad. Pushing her hair back out of her face, Ana marched across the center of the shelter. Brad was surrounded by Yanomami, but the tribe parted to allow her near him. She walked quickly to his side.

"Brad, you're okay! I thought—I was afraid you'd been strung up like those monkeys."

His blue eyes were hard to read. "Would you care?"

"Only if you turned up as the first course," she shot back.

"You think I'd be too tough to eat?" He sounded almost lighthearted.

But Ana looked past him and saw an empty hammock where the little girl had lain. Fear blossomed inside her. "Brad! Did she die?"

Even as he shook his head, she located the little girl in her mother's arms. The Yanomami were smiling, and she saw why. The girl was drinking water from a gourd; she definitely looked stronger. And the other two children looked better, too, less feverish, their eyes clearer.

Brad winked at her. "Don't look for me on the menu just yet."

The little girl's mother spoke eagerly to Brad.

"She says the evil spirits have departed," he

translated to Ana. "And that the pinprick was good."

Then Maleo spoke again, laughing heartily, and some of the other tribespeople spoke rapidly in their staccato rhythm.

"What are they saying?" Ana asked.

"They've decided to celebrate the children's improvement," Brad told her. "We're invited to a feast."

"Oh, great. Fried monkey this time?" Ana said weakly.

Brad laughed. "Let's go find you some fruit. At this rate, you'll appreciate my granola bars."

Watching several women check an armadillo, still in its armored skin and hung to smoke over a fire, Ana agreed quickly. She wasn't sure she was up to the Yanomamis' idea of gourmet delights.

As she and Brad walked back across the yano to their own fireside, she asked, remembering his skill with the syringes the night before, "Where did you learn to do that—give injections, and all?"

"My mother," Brad told her.

"I thought you said she was a botanist." Ana drank from her water bottle, then accepted two large bananas from a smiling Yanomami child and tossed one to Brad. Peeling the banana, she bit into the smooth, sweet fruit.

Quickly Brad peeled his and took a bite. "She

is. But she learned a lot from my dad; he was a physician."

"Was?"

"He died when I was twelve, trying to save a child caught in a collapsed building."

"Oh, Brad, I'm sorry," Ana said, seeing this new facet of him for the first time. Maybe she and Brad had something in common—an absent father—though from different reasons.

Brad nodded slowly. "I still miss him. But at least I know his life stood for something."

Instantly Ana was on the defensive. "You mean, unlike my dad?" She sat up straighter, glaring at Brad.

"Touchy, aren't you?" Brad raised his brows. "Who said anything about your father?"

"You've made your opinions clear enough. But you're wrong; my father's not a crook, and he's not raping the rain forest. I'm going to prove it to you before we're through." Ana blinked hard; she turned away before Brad could see the tears in her eyes.

"Ana," he said, "I didn't mean . . ."

But she stared stubbornly away from him, not wanting him to see just how much anxiety she felt about her father. If only she could find Jose Puentes; if only she had the chance to prove her father's innocence.

Struggling with the emotions churning inside her, Ana almost didn't hear Brad's quiet comment.

"I hope you're not disappointed."

Why was his tone so somber? He sounded so sure of his knowledge. In fact, Ana reflected bitterly, he sounded more sure of what he *knew* about her father than she *felt* she knew about Jose Puentes.

Suddenly, she didn't want to be so close to Brad. Ana stood up and walked across the compound, glancing at a Yanomami woman preparing her husband for the celebration. Using a stick dipped in red dye, she was marking him with large spots and other designs.

Other women were drawing streaks and wavy lines on their husbands' or their own bodies. One man carefully added bird down to his hair, until he seemed to be wearing a fluffy white cap.

Ana stared at the woman at the next fire, who added fresh flowers to her armbands; the woman already had thin slivers of wood protruding from her lip.

The man in the next hammock wore green and yellow parrot feathers through his ears.

"I feel downright underdressed," Ana murmured.

Groups of children ran and played in the center of the yano. One little boy clambered up a pole, agile as a monkey. Then Ana saw that a small girl at the fringe of the group was watching her.

Ana smiled at the youngster, who had liquid brown eyes and looked about four years old. The little girl, who wore only red armbands, giggled in response. She was bedecked for the coming party too. Leaves and flowers were tucked into her armbands, and she wore white flowers through her small earlobes.

Ana looked more closely. There, in the midst of the green leaves and white and yellow flowers of the armbands, she saw a fragment of blue that looked different in texture, and the color was strangely familiar.

"Brad," she called to him, forgetting her anger. "Look at this."

He walked across to join her. "What is it?"

"Ask her if I can see her armband." Ana motioned to the bright-eyed little girl.

Brad spoke briefly; the child seemed hesitant.

Ana went back to her backpack. She found a tube of lipstick and brought it over. "Look, tell her I'll trade her for this; it'll make nice decorations. All I want is that piece of blue."

Brad translated, and the little girl, after watching Ana swivel the tube of pink lipstick, agreed eagerly. The child accepted her prize, twisting the pink tube first up, then down, while Brad removed the scrap of paper from her armband.

136

"What is it?" Brad handed the paper to Ana.

"It looks like the memo paper that my father's company uses—the color is always the same," Ana told him. "Yes, look!"

It was only part of a sheet, but she could make out most of the printed legend at the top: Puentes Industries. The handwriting was blurred, and the words were in Portuguese. Ana strained to decipher the message.

"What does it say?" Brad watched her, his dark brows raised.

"It looks like, oh—my father's name—I think it says, 'Puentes is coming, be ready. . . .' The rest is gone. but underneath this line, I can see another word."

"Well?"

"It says, 'Danger.' I told you something was wrong! My father's in trouble—I know it!"

Eleven

"Let's not jump to conclusions," Brad said reasonably, peering at the paper.

"I'm not. Brad, think of everything that we've seen or been through since I came. The dead guy, the abandoned camp, the missing chartered plane, those two guys who tried to hurt me . . ." Involuntarily Ana shivered, remembering. "Don't you see? It's a pattern. Now, please, ask her where she found this."

Still Brad looked doubtful. "That piece of paper could have been around for weeks," he pointed out.

"And it might not. Just ask her, will you?" Impatience sharpened the tone of her voice.

Brad spoke to the little girl again in her own tongue. The child spoke softly, pointing.

"It was on a trail down toward the river; she found it when she went to fetch water," Brad translated.

"Ask her to please show us." Ana stood up.

"Ana—"

"I have to see."

Brad shrugged, then spoke again. The child immediately trotted off toward the jungle, seeming to regard this as a game. Ana followed just behind her, with Brad on her heels.

Steadily they walked through the forest, following a well-worn trail. Soon Ana saw the flash of the river ahead, and the child slowed.

The little girl stopped near the bank, where foot-high roots of a towering tree protruded; she pointed. Ana saw a slight depression in the soil. Was that a footprint, still showing in the thin layer of leaves that covered the ground? Ana found a stick and poked through the brown leaves, looking for any other sign of her father's passing, but found nothing except several large beetles, which scurried away.

Ana straightened, sighing in frustration. "There's got to be something."

"That scrap of paper could have come from anywhere, carried on the wind," Brad said. "You're wasting your time. We should get back to camp."

Ana turned away from him, not wanting to admit that he might be right. She stared across the river, blinking back tears of disappointment that had lain close to the surface for days. She'd thought she had found a clue to her father's disappearance, but she was no closer to finding answers to all the questions that haunted her. Where was her father?

Suddenly a flash of light from across the river made her blink. Ana narrowed her eyes, following it. It was a reflection off a small bright object, but she couldn't identify the source before a cloud slid over the sun. She knew it was nothing natural to the jungle.

"Look, Brad." Quickly she ran down the bank closer to the water, but from her lower viewpoint, the shiny object had disappeared from view. Still, Ana knew it was there.

"We have to cross the river; there's something on the other side."

A look of impatience crossed Brad's face. "Ana, let's just go back."

"Why can't you give me a chance? Just once pretend you believe my story. How would you feel if you thought your mother was in danger?" Her jaw clenched, Ana turned to face Brad.

Wordlessly Brad pointed to the sky, visible from the riverbanks as it never was inside the forest itself. Vaguely, Ana had noticed that the light was dimming but hadn't given it much thought. Now she saw that heavy clouds had appeared, and the sky's color had changed from clear blue to dark slate. A sudden crash of thunder made her flinch, and the little Yanomami girl turned and ran for home.

"Ana, I'm not trying to be mean. But we need to get back to shelter. That's a major rainstorm coming."

But the thought of abandoning the one slim lead she'd found went against everything Ana knew. She simply couldn't. "No, I'm going across the river," she said with quiet determination. "But you don't have to come. Go back to the yano." A path of broken water plants and muddy footprints led her to Brad's canoe, hidden only a few feet away. In moments she had tossed the covering palm leaves aside.

"Ana, don't be silly," Brad said infuriatingly. "Wait until after the storm."

Without replying, Ana dragged the canoe to the water's edge. Brad started down the bank after her, as though only now realizing the seriousness of her intent.

Quickly she climbed into the small boat, settling deeply into the middle.

"Ana!"

As she pushed away from the shore with one of the paddles, she heard a splash, then felt the canoe rock when Brad jumped in behind her. But she didn't look around, bending to her paddling, sending them as straight as the current allowed to the other bank of the river.

Thunder boomed again, and lightning cracked in an almost straight line to a tree just beyond them. Ana gritted her teeth, wondering how much danger they were in on the open river, but she refused to turn back now.

"This is great," Brad muttered angrily behind her. She heard the quiet sound of his paddle working the water. "A good place to be in the middle of a lightning storm is in a little canoe on the *water*. We're all gonna die."

Fortunately, they had reached the halfway point, and Brad seemed to have decided that the far bank was their best hope. He paddled fiercely with her, and in another few minutes, Ana jumped out and helped him drag the canoe up from the water.

While Brad turned the canoe on its side to escape the coming rain, Ana hurried up the bank to find the gleaming metallic object she had glimpsed from the other side of the river.

In moments she came upon it, and the bitter disappointment almost made Ana choke. It was just a tin can, sitting on top of a pile of rubbish with beer cans, scraps of paper, and an empty whiskey bottle. Unremarkable signs of civilization in the jungle, Ana thought with disgust as she cautiously turned over the garbage.

"So was it worth risking a lightning bolt?" Brad's voice was angry. "Any minute now we're going to be soaked."

Intent on examining the pile, Ana ignored him. She found a few more fragments of blue memo paper, but to her frustration, she couldn't decipher any words.

"Someone connected with my father's company was here fairly recently, because the paper hasn't completely turned to pulp," she said thoughtfully.

"Maybe your father, on whatever mission took him away," Brad suggested without interest, scanning the area for possible shelter.

"No!" Ana stood up, dusting her hands. "My father would never have left this mess."

"How can you be sure?" Brad's brows lifted in a familiar gesture of skepticism; Ana struggled to hold on to her temper.

"When I was a kid, my father wouldn't let me throw a gum wrapper out the car window," she retorted. "Even in Rio, where the streets weren't exactly spotless. I know him. He'd never leave a pile of garbage like this, in the jungle or anywhere else."

Brad didn't look convinced.

Struggling to see in the gloomy light, Ana looked around; was that a bent twig? Had the unknown party gone this way? "I think I see where they headed," she told Brad.

"It's going to pour any second—we need to find a place to wait out the storm. Anyway, you can't go off into the forest; you'll just get lost. They probably continued down the river," Brad argued.

But Ana had already plunged into the thick growth of trees. Her excitement rose as she found first a vague footprint, then a cigarette stub crushed beneath someone's foot. She hurried forward, looking keenly at the ground.

Again she saw signs of someone's passage in the thick layer of leaves that coated the forest floor. With any luck, she could trace this guy to his camp. Maybe even discover who was behind the murders and the other happenings of the past few days.

To her surprise, she found that Brad was behind her. "I'm not turning back," she warned him.

He shrugged with exaggerated patience. "It's easier to follow you now than to find you when you get lost."

Despite his lack of faith, Ana was glad to have

him with her. Together, they searched the forest floor.

"There, I think," Ana said, and they moved farther into the jungle.

Slowly they traced the faint marks of passage for another hundred feet, while thunder rumbled overhead. Then came the deluge.

Ana heard the crash of falling rain against the leaves above them, and instants later, fat raindrops started splashing her face and arms. The rain fell in layers of wetness that hit her with chilling force. Gulping, Ana felt heavy rivulets run down her hair, soaking her light clothing.

The water fell in sheets, and Ana could barely see the big trees around them. Thunder crashed again, and even in the gloom of the forest, Ana found the glare of lightning etched against her eyelids—she blinked, trying to see.

"Get away from the trees," Brad yelled into her ear. He pulled her as far away from the forest giants as they could manage, crouching in the small open space as sheets of rainwater soaked them. Ana felt soggy strands of hair sticking to her forehead. Her T-shirt was sodden with water, lying cold and clammy against her skin, and her denim shorts seemed five pounds heavier. Her shoes were also waterlogged, and small rivers ran down her bare arms and legs, while water stung her eyes.

Brad crouched beside her, his arms around her shoulders. Ana leaned against him, shivering as cold showers of water continued to drench her, her teeth chattering even more when the thunder rolled and crashed above them, and a bolt of lightning exploded all too close, sending the top of a large tree crashing to the ground.

Her own arms around his neck, Ana held Brad even closer, glad that the noise of the storm precluded any "I-told-you-so's." Right now, she just wanted to live through this storm; then Brad could complain all he wanted. Crouching so close to the ground, she could smell the sweet-sour musty scent of sodden leaves and damp bark and muddy earth. Thunder roared again, and she buried her face in Brad's shoulder. If they lived through this, she would apologize to him, she really would.

It seemed like hours that they huddled together, barely able to see beyond their own drenched bodies, but Ana realized that the storm, in fact, was a brief one, washing itself out as quickly as it had blown up.

When the rain slowed to a steady patter, Brad removed one arm from her shoulders to touch her cheek. "You okay?"

His tone was gentle, not angry and accusing as she had expected.

Ana nodded, glad that the wetness of her cheeks would hide a tear or two of relief. "I'm sorry; I didn't know it could be like this."

"Rains a lot here." Standing up, Brad put out a hand to pull her to her feet. "But I think this storm's about done."

Ana's legs were stiff; she straightened with an effort. "Thank goodness."

"The tracks will have been washed away," he told her. "We might as well go back to camp and get some dry clothes."

Ana looked around at the dripping trees, the soggy leaves. She nodded, sighing. They would never find more trail signs after the violence of the storm.

After retracing their steps to the riverbank, they dumped out the water that had blown into the canoe and paddled back across the river.

On the other shore, Brad put protecting palm leaves over the canoe again; then they hiked back to camp. Ana's drenched clothes were soggy and uncomfortable against her skin. No wonder the Yanomami didn't wear clothing, she thought.

She felt thoroughly discouraged. She was never going to find her father. All the risks she had taken, all the discomfort she'd been through, and what had she gained? Nothing. She was just as lost, just as ignorant of her father's whereabouts as she'd been when she got off the plane.

When they reached the yano, some of the children laughed aloud at their bedraggled appearance. Brad shooed the youngsters away and turned his back so she could pull off her soggy clothes. She rummaged through her pack for her other set and donned them with relief. Combing her damp hair away from her face, Ana felt despair still too near the surface. She needed some time alone.

Picking up her dripping clothes, she told Brad, "Give me your wet things; I'll take them to the river with mine and rinse them out."

He looked at her in surprise.

"It was my fault you got soaked," Ana explained, her voice listless even to her own ears.

"Okay, thanks." He looked at her thoughtfully.

At the river's edge she knelt and dunked the clothing into the dark water. At last she could let the tears come, with no one to see. What should she do? Admit defeat and go home?

No. There was no way she could desert her father now, like this. The letter he'd written was in her pack at the Yanomami camp, but Ana knew it by heart; she had read it so many times.

149

Can you ever forgive me, Ana? Will you give me another chance?

Only if she found him first.

"I haven't done much to help, Dad," she said aloud. "I'm trying, but I'm not very good at this."

She scrubbed the clothing, rinsing and wringing out the garments. While she pounded them against a flat rock by the bank, Ana remembered the gleaming laundry room in her mother's Manhattan apartment—the washing machine with its different cycles and water temperatures, the dryer with its shiny dials. She shook her head. This was unreal. All she needed now were red streaks on her forehead and a lot less clothing. "Paradise," she told herself, "has its drawbacks."

At least she'd stopped crying. After wiping her face on her wet T-shirt, she took the armload of damp clothing back to the yano. There she hung it over the hammock strings to dry close to the fire.

Brad didn't comment on her red face or swollen eyes, but he had a surprise waiting for her. He had accepted several small fish from a returning fisherman's catch, cleaned them, then grilled them on a stick over the fire. "I know how much you love fried monkey, but I thought you could use a change," he told her. "Here, try this."

The savory smell lightened her spirits a little, and her mouth watered. She accepted the small, crisp fish eagerly, burning her lip on the first bite.

"Ouch." Blowing gently on the tender flesh, Ana ate more carefully. "Tastes good. What is it?"

"Piranha," Brad told her.

Ana almost dropped her dinner. "You're kidding, right?"

"No, it's good eating." Brad bit into a second little fish that he had cooked over the glowing coals. "Tomi's a great fisherman."

The headman lounged in his hammock, waiting for his wife to finish preparations for the feast. Ana noticed for the first time that Tomi was missing two toes on his right foot, the scars long healed.

"Piranha?" she asked Brad weakly.

He nodded, taking another bite of fish.

"Oh, what the heck," Ana murmured. She finished the fish, trying not to think about its savage habits, and threw the bones into the fire.

The young measles victims had continued to improve, and the mood in the village was exultant. Oddly, it made Ana feel even more despondent and more alone. She watched the women prepare thick yellow plantain soup in a trench made from a hollowed-out log. The party menu also included monkeys and the smoked armadillo, and other things like caterpillars wrapped in green leaves that Ana didn't inspect too closely.

The villagers ate until they were obviously gorged.

Alone in her hammock, Ana felt lost in the gloom. In the next hammock, Brad watched the dancers at the center of the yano acting out stories.

Looking at Brad in the fading light, Ana saw him frown suddenly.

"What is it?"

"They're talking about a threat to the rain forest. Something is 'killing the jungle,' but I don't understand what they mean," he told her.

Ana shook her head. Great. Another mystery.

Swinging out of her hammock, she headed for an opening in the yano. Her fears for her father, her disappointment in her own attempts to find him—she was thoroughly discouraged. And the brown-skinned people around her, the rapid chatter, the shrill laughter, the smell of strange foods—it all seemed alien and overwhelming.

She bent to walk beneath the outside layer of leaves and thatch and stood outside, alone in the tropical darkness.

Somewhere an animal shrieked, and she heard the repetitive call of birds. Ana stared blindly out at the darkness, her arms folded against her chest. Somewhere out there in the black jungle night was her father. And he needed her help.

152

"Ana?" Brad had followed her.

Her throat seemed to close; she couldn't answer.

When he touched her shoulder gently, her defenses melted, and Ana turned to lean against him, this time with no excuse except the almost overpowering loneliness she felt. "My father's in trouble, Brad," she whispered. "And I haven't been able to help him. I've blown it."

Brad held her, his arms strong and comforting. For a long minute, she lay her face against his bare chest, feeling his heart pound beneath her cheek. She could almost think Brad cared.

But his next words made her stiffen. "Giving up, city girl? The jungle too tough for you?"

She pulled back, anger replacing her despair. Standing up very straight, Ana glared at him through the darkness. "No, I'm not. I'll find my father. With your help or without it."

Twelve

"That's more like it," Brad answered. "At least you're snapping at me again."

His wry tone confused her. Ana tried to see his expression through the thick tropical darkness. "Brad—just tell me the truth. Do you believe me about my father being in trouble or not?"

The night air was silent for a moment as Brad considered. "I just think it would be easy to be wrong about things. There could be other explanations. Like the dead man. He could have been asleep, drunk, ill—you said you never touched him."

"Brad, he smelled."

"So he needed a bath."

"What about the disappearance of the airfield chief?"

"That's common enough; people out here get tired of working in the middle of nowhere, get lonesome for home and family, or just want to party for a while. He could have hitched a ride with a supply plane. Maybe he's already back by now."

"What about the two men who assaulted me? Or do you think I made up this bruise, too?" Ana couldn't see his eyes clearly, but she saw Brad frown.

"There are some rough types in the jungle."

"Brad, I'm really worried. What if my father's been kidnapped? He's very rich. They could be holding him somewhere, waiting for ransom." Ana swallowed hard, trying to control her fears.

But to her surprise, Brad shook his head. "He's not a victim. Your father is involved in whatever shady deal his company is up to."

"I don't believe you! My father's a business-man, but he's honest. He doesn't break the law."

"It's the truth, Ana. I can prove it."

Ana wanted to shout at him, but sudden doubt made her bite back the angry words.

"Show me," she said tersely, and followed him back to the yano.

When they reached their own fire, Brad bur-rowed into his pack and came out with a folded sheet she recognized.

"That's the map you took from my father's camp," she said, her tone accusing.

Brad nodded. "Look." He unfolded it and held it close to the flickering fire. "The photos show the beginnings of a mine, and look at this."

Ana tried to read the symbols he indicated, but they made little sense to her. "What does it mean?"

"It's a geological survey of this part of the Amazon Basin, and there are some locations marked. It was commissioned by Puentes Industries. There's no doubt about that; your father's signature is at the bottom."

Ana stared hard at the wavy signature in the dim light; yes, it looked like her father's handwriting. "Why are these areas marked in red?" she asked, tracing the lower part of the sheet with one finger.

Brad looked up at her, his blue eyes sober. "I think they're hunting for gold."

"Gold?" Ana said in surprise, her voice too loud. She glanced around as if someone might overhear, but the Yanomami were still absorbed in their celebrating, and she had spoken in English.

Brad nodded. "The rain forest isn't suited for most farming or ranching, and even lumber doesn't pay well, though it's often tried. But this area is rich in minerals, and some people don't mind destroying the tribes, the trees, the whole ecological system to get to underground riches. Outlaw gold miners have been a problem for years, though the government now tries to protect at least part of the rain forest for the tribes. I'm afraid this map may show a secret mine; I took it to show the authorities."

Ana gripped her arms tightly, hugging herself against renewed anxiety. "Can we find this place? See if my father's there?"

"Ana, it could be dangerous. I might try it if I were alone, but I'm not dragging you through the jungle."

"But my father—"

"If your father is there, he may be trying to keep you away for a reason. Maybe he wants to protect you from the truth," Brad told her.

Ana covered her face with her hands. Was this to be the end of the new beginning her father had promised? She remembered her dad returning home after another long day at the office, the smell of the city clinging to him as he leaned over the half-sleeping Ana to kiss her good night. There had been a gentleness there—she hadn't imagined it. Could the same man be a ruthless exploiter of the rain forest?

Brad touched her shoulder, and she tensed.

"Look, I'm sorry I have to tell you this. It's a drag, learning your own father's one of the bad guys. But you can't walk into trouble, Ana. Go back to the city. If your father wants to see you, he'll know where to contact you. In the morning, we'll start for my mother's camp. You can use the radio there to get a plane."

He reached out for her, but Ana turned away. She couldn't accept comfort from someone who had just accused her father of ruthless destruction. Wrapping herself in a blanket, she turned her back to Brad and climbed stiffly into her hammock.

She heard the rustle of paper as he returned the map to his pack, then the creak of the wooden poles as he lay down in his own hammock. He was only a foot away, yet it might have been a mile. The closeness she had briefly imagined outside the yano seemed only a memory.

Ana stared into the dark sky beyond the open center of the yano until the last native fell asleep, the fires burned down to ashes, and only the crickets called. For what seemed like hours, she racked her brains over mysterious maps and illicit gold mines until, close to morning, she finally fell asleep.

*　　　*　　　*

The next morning they repacked their back-packs in silence, Ana taking some of Brad's medical supplies so he had room for plant specimens he had gathered for his mother. Then they said good-bye to the Yanomami. Tomi, the headman, and the parents of the ill children made fervent speeches, and a procession of natives escorted them to the river and Brad's canoe.

Looking over her shoulder as they floated down the river, Ana murmured, "I won't ever forget them, Tomi and his tribe."

"That's not his real name, actually," Brad told her, bending to dip his paddle into the water. "If you knew his Yanomami name, you'd have power over him. An enemy could shout it in battle, to bring bad luck to him. So I give them nicknames that won't offend anyone."

Ana, who had begun to think she understood the forest tribe, shook her head. The canoe slipped easily through the blackish water, going with the flow of the river this time as they headed downstream, so paddling was easy.

The small rapids that had looked so alarming to Ana the first time seemed almost uneventful; they made their way around the rolling currents without problems, then floated on down the river.

In the middle of the afternoon, Brad aimed the little boat toward the bank.

"Why are we stopping?" Ana helped him pull the canoe up on dry land and cover it with palm leaves.

Brad glanced at her, but she refused to meet his gaze. He might think she was leaving meekly, but after a long night struggling with doubts about her father, Ana was sure she wasn't ready to run away, not till she knew the truth. And despite what Brad thought, she didn't believe they had uncovered the whole story.

"Big rapids downstream," he explained. "We have to go on foot for a ways."

Ana bit back a groan of impatience. If Brad said the rapids were big, they must be big.

Unerringly Brad found the trail, showing her a slash on a tree trunk that marked the path. They shouldered their packs and set off once again through the hushed green dimness of the rain forest.

About an hour before sunset, the always heavy humidity grew even more intense; the jungle felt like a steam bath, Ana thought, rubbing her damp forehead.

"It's going to rain," Brad told her. "We'd better put up a shelter for the night."

Working in a silent truce, Ana helped him construct another simple structure like the one they'd shared the first night they had spent together in the jungle. Finding young trees of the right diameter, Brad cut three long, sturdy poles. These he pushed into the earth in a triangular form. While he used lianas to lash more branches to form a skeleton roof, Ana gathered large banana leaves to lay across the top to keep off the rain.

With Brad's machete, she cut and gathered an armload of leaves. On her way back to the shelter, Ana detected a whisper of movement in the tree above her. She froze then relaxed as she identified what had first appeared to be the stump of a tree bough. The odd-shaped animal, now motionless again as if it detected her surveillance, had shaggy fur green-dotted with algae and was as inoffensive as any creature she might find in the forest.

Ana gazed up at the blunt-faced animal, smiling slowly at an old memory. Her father had pointed out the first sloth she'd ever seen, when she'd been about six. She'd almost forgotten that afternoon, the side trip they had taken through a tree-lined park on the way back from one of her dad's factories. How could she forget the good moments and remember only the times he had let her down?

She wouldn't give up on her dad, not yet.

"Anything wrong?" Brad had come to find her.

"No," Ana told him, still smiling. "Just saw an old friend."

He looked quizzical, but she didn't explain. Together they finished the shelter barely in time; without the warning of thunder, a sudden deluge descended. Rain fell in sheets, and all around them, the tall trees glistened with wetness.

The simple Yanomami-style shelter kept off most of the rain. They had hung their hammocks from the poles, and Ana lay watching the rain fall, feeling only occasional drops blow under their green roof.

Kneeling, Brad took packets of trail mix and some bananas from his pack. He held out her share of the food, then hesitated.

Looking up at him, she was suddenly very aware of his clear blue eyes and rugged chin, of raindrops glistening on his tanned chest. His closeness triggered a response inside her. She had to force herself to look down, to take the food and not let her hand tremble.

They ate in silence, but there was an increased tension in the air that didn't come from the storm. Later, when they climbed into their hammocks, closer together than they had been even in the yano, Ana found it hard to relax. She was too aware of him in his own hammock, lying too still, breathing too quickly to be asleep. Did Brad feel it, also, the catch in the throat when he came near her, the warmth of his skin that left her rigid with repressed emotions?

But it was impossible. He thought her father was a criminal, and that she was a spoiled city girl. What kind of relationship could she have with Brad? Their worlds were completely different. *They* were completely different.

"Are you going to do this the rest of your life?" she asked him suddenly. It seemed easy to be blunt when they lay so close in the dark, alone.

"What?" he answered.

"Live here, in the rain forest. Work with your mom. Help the native tribes."

"Frankly," Brad said, "I can't think of anything more important for me to do. As a botanist, my mom just might discover a plant that could save the lives of thousands of people. Or a plant that produces an environmentally safe dye for cloth. Or one whose extract could be a new major source of fuel. There's a whole medicine chest, a whole chemical factory, right in front of us, and it's being wiped out before we have time to find out what one hundredth of these plants can do."

Ana lay in her hammock, quietly digesting this information. When he put it that way, his work sounded noble and important. But the reality of his life—his living conditions, the food he ate, the clothes he wore—all added up to something foreign, uncomfortable, a little frightening.

"Then why don't you go back to the States, go to college? If you got a degree . . . if you were a botanist like your mother, you could do more here than just collect plant samples for your mom."

"I'm already in college. Next year I'll be a junior."

"You are?" Ana twisted in her hammock, trying to see him, but the night was too dark. She heard amusement in his tone when he answered.

"I'm on special leave from UCLA to do field studies. Also, I admit I wanted to keep an eye on my mom. The area has seen outbreaks of trouble, as you've noticed. What's wrong? Didn't think I had it in me to get into a good school?"

"No—it's not that," she protested quickly. *Well, it's sort of that,* she admitted silently to herself. "It's just that you seem so completely at home here, in the jungle. I'm having a hard time imagining you on a college campus, mingling with other students, hanging out in the library," she said. "Why didn't you tell me before?"

Brad laughed. "You made up your mind about me the first time you saw me—you thought I was a jungle bum. I was just playing along. Next time, beware of stereotypes."

"Speaking of stereotypes, you're convinced that I'm exactly like what you *think* my father is," she pointed out. "And you think he'll stop at nothing to get what he wants—even if it means destroying the rain forest. Despite all the evidence right in front of your eyes, you refuse to believe that he might be just a businessman, running an honest company, who got caught up in something beyond his control. You refuse to believe that he's in trouble, that he may be hurt. Not too open-minded of you, Brad Eliot," she finished with quiet passion.

The silence stretched; it seemed thick with emotion. "I get so angry at some of the waste that goes on here, it was easy to blame your dad," Brad said slowly. "But you're making me think again, Ana."

Ana had to blink hard. "Thanks," she whispered. She felt, as much as saw, him put out his hand in the darkness, and she twisted her body so she could put out her own hand to meet his. The warmth of his touch, the strength of his grip, she could almost feel a thrill of delight run through her whole body.

Ana held tight to his hand, then felt him lift her hand to his lips, kiss her palm, gently. For a moment the warm, humid darkness seemed to sing with more than the chatter of wild things.

She wanted to turn into his arms, but the hammock swayed dangerously, and Ana thought she might tip out. She dropped his hand to cling to the side of the hammock, but the metaphor was almost too fitting. Their frail first step toward a relationship was balanced so precariously; would it ever have a chance to develop, or would the answers to all Ana's questions reveal not just her father's guilt but an end to their feelings for each other?

It seemed hours before she finally drifted into an uneasy sleep.

The next morning they ate, broke camp quickly, and headed out again. By noon they had come back to a river and soon reached the out-skirts of a clearing. Ana saw movement in the shadows.

Brad called to a native bending over a recent catch of fish. "Arabu!"

It was the same man who had rescued her from the two men at the airfield, Ana realized. She smiled warmly at him and followed as Brad and Arabu walked to a nearby camp.

"About time you got back; I was getting wor-ried." A tall woman with dark hair peppered lightly with gray strode forward. Dressed in khaki shorts and shirt, she greeted Brad with a quick hug.

"Had a few detours, but all's well," Brad said cheerfully.

His mother shook her head, then turned to Ana. "And who is this?"

Brad said, "Mom, this is Ana Puentes. She's sort of stranded; she needs to radio for a plane. My mother, Dr. Emily Eliot."

Forcing a nervous smile, Ana said, "Hello. I was so glad to run into Brad. He really helped me over the last few days—I would have died without him." With a shock, Ana realized her polite words may very well be true.

Dr. Eliot seemed brisk and no-nonsense, and Ana waited to see if she would have the same reaction as Brad had to the Puentes name.

But Emily Eliot looked at her searchingly, then held out her hand. "Welcome to our camp."

"Thank you," Ana said gratefully. Dr. Eliot's clasp was unexpectedly strong.

"There's soup cooking over the fire. Come along—you must be hungry."

"Actually, could I radio about my dad first, Dr. Eliot?" Ana asked, her voice husky with emotion. "I haven't quite convinced Brad, but I think my father's been kidnapped. He was supposed to meet me and he didn't, and he wasn't at his camp—no one was."

At least no one alive, she thought, but she couldn't explain everything; it was too complicated, and she was tired of having people doubt her stories.

Emily Eliot raised her brows in a gesture much like her son's. "I can see why you're concerned. Come along; we'll show you the radio. And call me Emily—everyone does."

As they walked, Ana glanced at the tents and huts that made up the Eliots' camp. She saw long thatch shelters holding roughly built racks with dozens of neatly labeled plant specimens, and small but powerful-looking microscopes, even a battery-powered laptop computer.

"Deforestation of the rain forest destroys about seventeen thousand species of plants and animals every year—such a waste." Emily waved toward the tents. "We're doing what we can, but it's like scooping up the ocean in a teacup, and seeing the ocean dry up even as we speak."

There was nothing Ana could say to this.

After another few moments, Emily waved her hand at a small canvas tent. "Here's the radio tent. Brad will help you report your worries to the authorities, Ana. And they'll see about getting you a plane."

Watching Brad as he competently handled the controls of the shortwave radio set, Ana tried to marshal all her persuasive powers. When Brad connected Ana with a government official in Manaus, she had to clear her throat nervously. Earnestly she launched into her story, trying to speak clearly and calmly, hoping the man wouldn't think she was crazy. No one at Puentes Industries had reported her father missing, but Ana insisted that a search be organized. She also had a telegram sent to her mother in New York, telling her she was safe and would call soon.

After the official had taken down her story, she arranged for a plane to pick her up at the Eliots' camp. She herself would go to Manaus, Ana decided. In person, she could do more to make sure the search for her father was given high priority. The thought of leaving Brad gave her an unexpected pang, but she had no choice. Ana had to find her father. There were so many unanswered questions: Was he alive? Was his company involved in deforestation? Why had he disappeared? Lastly, and most important, did he truly care about her? Was that why he had written?

It was their last hope, and Ana's final act of faith. With all that at stake, she couldn't be distracted by Brad's blue eyes, or by his doubts.

When Ana finished, and Brad signed off, he looked up at her gravely. Emily Eliot had gone to examine the newest plant samples, and to see about a meal for them. The plane Ana had requested would take several hours to arrive.

"Hungry?" Brad asked. "We're out of stewed monkey, but we can rustle up something."

She grinned reluctantly. "I'm starved, but I'd like a bath even more, if you don't mind."

"Sounds good to me, too."

He showed her a primitive but effective shower rigged up beneath a tin rain reservoir, and found her a pair of his denim cutoffs and a T-shirt donated by his mother.

After a thorough scrub, Ana felt deliciously clean. She was sitting on a camp stool in the tent Emily had offered, combing her damp hair, when Brad came in. He too had washed and changed, the stubble on his chin gone. He looked almost civilized, she realized a little giddily. She was surprised when he hesitated in front of her.

"Ana, what you said last night—I just wanted to tell you. I'll do everything I can to find your father while you're gone."

The declaration took her breath away. Ana jumped to her feet, putting her hand on his arm unconsciously. "Brad, what made you change your mind?"

"I'm not saying your dad is innocent. But you're right—I shouldn't judge him till all the evidence is in. If he doesn't deserve that much, you do."

His expression was serious, and it blurred a little in her sight. Ana blinked hard, swallowing the tears of relief.

"That means a lot to me, Brad. Thank you."

Covering her hand with his own, he said, "I guess I jump to conclusions sometimes, and then I'm too stubborn to admit my mistakes. Like thinking you couldn't cope with the jungle, just because you're a city girl. You've done pretty well for yourself. I couldn't believe it when you said you bit that guy to escape. That took real guts."

For the first time, Ana thought there was respect in his gaze, and it warmed her to the core. Without thinking, she lifted her face to his, her heart soaring, and he leaned down, meeting her lips with his own.

The kiss began gently. Ana shut her eyes and enjoyed the tenderness of his touch. Then, forgetting her anxieties, aware only of the moment and Brad's nearness, she kissed him more urgently. His touch became demanding, his grip on her arms tightened.

Ana felt her pulse jump. No one had ever kissed her like this. Sliding her arms around his neck, she pulled him even closer. Their bodies seemed to melt together, and Ana had no wish to pull back. The camp, the meal that awaited them—all seemed far away.

But a new, harsh roar intruded. Ana felt Brad stiffen; then she too pulled back to listen.

"Come on—let's get to the airfield," Brad told her, frowning.

Surely the plane hadn't arrived already. She and Brad ran past the tents, joined by Emily Eliot and two natives as they neared the grassy strip on the edge of the camp.

With a steady throbbing noise, a helicopter came into view, then lowered itself to the grass with a whirl of its pinions.

Ana blinked at the blast of wind the chopper stirred up. A man stepped out of the chopper before its rotors stopped spinning, and her eyes widened in surprise.

"Raoul!"

Thirteen

"Raoul, what are you doing here?" Ana asked, too surprised to say anything else. "How did you know where I was?"

"We picked up your radio message," Raoul told her, his smile wide. "Ana, I was so worried when you didn't return. Then we couldn't contact the airfield. What happened?"

"I wish I knew." Ana shook Raoul's out-stretched hand, relieved to have a new ally. She turned to introduce him to Brad and saw Brad frown.

"You always eavesdrop on other people's conversations?" Brad asked bluntly.

Raoul's glance was scathing. "It was a fortunate accident. I have been very concerned about Ana."

Ana said quickly, "But how did you get here from Rio so quickly?"

"Ah, I was not in the city. I was on my way to the Puentes camp, so we came here instead."

Ana didn't have time to worry about Brad's instant dislike of her father's assistant. "Raoul, my father's not at the camp. He seems to have disappeared. You must take me to Manaus—I want to organize a search."

"I know, Ana. I'm very distressed also. I've been told that your father and his men went out into the jungle and have not returned. I was on my way to his last camp, farther north than the one near the airfield. I may learn something there. But when we intercepted your message, I felt your father would wish me to check on you."

"I'm going with you," Ana decided. "We have to find him, Raoul. I knew something was wrong."

He nodded. "We must leave at once. I don't want to waste any more time."

"Ana," Brad interrupted, "I don't think this is such a good idea, rushing off like this. You radioed for a plane, remember? You should go to Manaus first and get more help. Contact the authorities."

"I have already done that," Raoul told him. "But I could not sit still while my employer is missing."

"Neither will I," Ana agreed. "Brad, don't you

see how lucky this is? A helicopter is much more maneuverable than a plane in the rain forest. Besides, as Raoul says, we may find a lead at the other camp."

Taking her arm, Brad pulled Ana several feet away, then spoke, keeping his voice low. "How do you know you can trust this guy?" he demanded.

Ana bit her lip, looking into the earnest blue eyes. Their kiss, their new understanding, meant a lot to her, but she couldn't allow Brad to delay her now. "Raoul works for my father, Brad. I've known him since I was a little girl. There's no need to worry. I have to go."

Coming up behind them as if he guessed Brad's objections, Raoul said, "The young lady will be well taken care of."

Emily Eliot, who had come up in time to hear the last part of the argument, said, "Radio us when you arrive at the camp, Ana, and let us know if you have any news."

"Of course. And thank you so much for everything," Ana told her. "I wish I had time to tell you how much it meant to me."

Arabu had brought her backpack; Ana smiled at the native. "Thank you for saving my life," she told him. Ana picked up her backpack and turned toward the chopper, pausing for an instant to look into Brad's frowning face. "Thanks for taking a chance on me, Brad," she told him. "You kept me alive in the jungle."

"I hope it wasn't wasted effort," he murmured, his dark brows still scowling.

Why did he have to be so stubborn? She'd talk to him later, Ana thought, after her father had been found. Right now, she had no time to argue.

"See you," she told him, wishing she could kiss him good-bye. But Raoul, Emily, and two natives were all there staring, and Brad himself looked stormy.

Sighing, Ana hurried to the helicopter. Raoul helped her in. It was a small craft, with boxes cluttering the passenger space. There was a pilot, and one other man, his eyes hidden by dark glasses, beside him. Ana and Raoul took seats in the rear and fastened their seat belts. Then the motor roared into higher gear. They lifted up smoothly, and Ana stared down at the camp. Brad stood watching them, his hair blown back by the fierce currents from the chopper, until they soared away over the thick green treetops.

"Do you know where my father was going when he disappeared?" Ana yelled at Raoul, trying to make herself heard over the whine of the engine.

Raoul made an expressive gesture with his

well-manicured hands. "I don't know very much. I received only a brief message. I've been very concerned—first unable to find you, and then your father disappearing. I was so glad to hear your voice on the radio, Ana. Did the mad scientist treat you well? I have heard rumors of her from the natives."

"Emily was very kind," Ana said a little stiffly. "She's not mad at all, just committed to an important cause. I've learned a lot about the rain forest."

"And her rude son, did you learn from him, too?"

Ana blinked, wondering if Raoul's English was good enough to understand what he had just suggested. With some effort she kept her expression bland, remembering how she and Brad had traded insults in the jungle, how furious he had made her—and how tender his kiss had been. She felt like a different person from the Ana Puentes who had plunged into the wilderness, and part of that was because of Brad.

"He's not rude," she said at last. "He just says what he thinks—very American."

Raoul looked unimpressed, smoothing his spotless French cuffs, and Ana tried not to smile. She could smell the heavy cologne that Raoul wore. No longer a gawky teenager, Raoul possessed a sexy Latin charm that most girls would swoon over. Yet compared to Brad's rugged appeal, Raoul looked too civilized, too well pressed. She couldn't imagine Raoul building a shelter in the middle of a jungle or paddling a canoe through dangerous rapids. Nor, she realized suddenly, could she picture him risking his life to help a native child.

But that wasn't fair. Raoul had, after all, come into the jungle to search for her father, hadn't he, and taken a detour to check on her as well? And he'd warned her against coming; he probably disliked the Amazon intensely. He certainly looked out of place here, with his city clothes and carefully combed hair.

"I hope we can find him soon," Raoul said now.

Ana nodded, sighing as she thought of her father. At least she knew now some of the delay had been out of his control. She prayed for the thousandth time that he wasn't hurt. But why had he gone into the jungle at all, when he had promised to meet her at the airport? There were still matters to settle between them.

Trying to block out images of her father lost in the jungle, ill or in pain, Ana watched the trees as they flew over them. She looked for the occasional movement of monkeys in the treetops, the bright exotic colors of orchids growing high on the jungle canopy. Raoul removed some papers from his briefcase and didn't talk during the noisy chopper ride.

Around them, clouds had gathered, hiding the sun. Ana hoped that they would reach their destination before a storm hit. The loss of the sun also confused her as to their direction, and the green layer of treetops beneath them was no help, one mile looking much like the next.

Were they crossing terrain that she and Brad had hiked so laboriously? If so, the helicopter took them much more swiftly. Ana thought she saw the airfield, but it passed on the edge of her vision and she couldn't be sure.

It was not long until the chopper began to circle, and she saw a small clearing with a few huts. Eagerly she peered down as the chopper landed, blowing up a cloud of dust as it neared the ground.

"We're here," Raoul told her. He had put away his papers. His only concession to the heat of the afternoon was to loosen his silk tie and remove his jacket. Opening the door of the chopper, he stepped out, waiting to help Ana down. With her backpack over her shoulder, she followed, looking around.

The camp with its thatch huts had a neglected look, weeds growing between the huts and a pile of garbage to the rear. Two khaki-clad men emerged to greet them, but neither was familiar to Ana. The first man leaned forward to speak to Raoul, but with the roar of the helicopter behind her, its motor still running, Ana couldn't make out what he was saying.

Raoul nodded to the man and motioned Ana to follow. She entered the tent eagerly, hoping for a positive sign. But except for a few boxes and the usual hammock, it was empty.

"Have they heard anything?"

Raoul shook his head. "No news yet, Ana. I'm sending out more men. You must be patient."

Ana sighed, and Raoul patted her shoulder. "Don't worry; we mustn't give up hope. Would you like to radio to the lady scientist and tell her you've arrived?"

It was the obvious thing to do, yet Ana hesitated. "I'll wait a while. We might hear something of my father," she decided. "They'll want to know."

"As you wish." Raoul spoke to the man behind them. "I'll see that you have something to eat; then you can rest. You must be tired."

Ana frowned, but she said politely, "Thank you, Raoul." If Raoul had brought her here only to treat her like a fragile flower, kept protected and out of the way, he'd soon find he was mistaken. But she didn't want to start arguing already, not with so many worries about her father still crowding her mind.

The surly assistant brought her a tin plate of canned stew and some bottled water. Ana should have been hungry, but she only picked at the food.

Where was her father? She wanted to dash out into the jungle to find him, but she knew that was foolish. She had no idea where to begin looking, and getting lost herself wouldn't help.

The afternoon seemed to stretch on forever. Raoul had disappeared, and Ana was in no mood to nap. She paced up and down the tent, then glanced outside. A short man walked across the camp. She knew him at once.

Ana tried not to scream. It was the second man from the airfield, the shorter one with the mustache who had run away when Arabu put an arrow into his partner.

Why was he here? Was he part of the plot against her father? Raoul should be warned.

After she watched the man head away from the camp and into the jungle, Ana picked up her pack and slipped out of the tent. Where was Raoul? She didn't have time to find him; the man would get away.

Brad would say this wasn't the smartest move, Ana thought. Brad was probably right, but she wasn't going to let a potential lead get away.

At the edge of the woods, Ana looked for a trail. She saw the faint marks of passage first, then found a slash on the tree trunk, just as Brad had shown her. This was the way the mustached man had gone.

After her days in the jungle, Ana found the trail easy to follow. It was quiet under the trees, and in the usual dim light she looked carefully for the slashes. She walked as silently as possible; she had learned a few things in all those miles she'd hiked beside Brad.

Just as she wondered if she should turn back, she saw a hut ahead of her with a man at the door. It wasn't the mustached man, but a larger one, yawning in the afternoon heat.

A guard—but what, or who, was he guarding? While she debated, Ana realized that the man had seen her through the trees.

She wouldn't retreat. Marching up to the hut, she faced the man boldly. "Raoul sent me," she told him in Portuguese.

While he blinked at her in surprise, Ana slipped around him and into the hut. The light was dim inside; the one window was covered with a piece of canvas. In a low-slung hammock in the far corner, Ana saw a man lying very still.

"Dad!" She ran forward, dropped to her knees, her heart beating fast. *Please let him be all right!*

Ana prayed silently. *Oh, God, make him be all right.*

He stirred. Ana found she had been holding her breath, and she gasped in relief. Reaching for his hand, she said, "Dad, it's Ana. Can you talk? How do you feel?"

As her eyes adjusted to the dimness, she saw him more clearly, and she couldn't suppress a start of surprise. She had never seen her father dirty; he was always meticulously groomed, his dark hair in place, his clothes neat. He had always seemed so strong, so much in command.

The man who lay in the hammock looked feverish, his face was covered with uneven stubble, and his shirt was torn and stained. But apart from his overall disheveled appearance, he looked so frail that Ana was shaken.

It was like seeing a great oak tree reduced to broken splinters. In her mind, Ana knew that anyone could fall ill, everyone must grow old. But in her heart, she had never expected to see her strong, powerful father, who could lift a giggling toddler with one hand, look so weak. Ana swallowed hard. Her father stared as if he didn't quite believe his eyes. "Ana, little one, is that really you? How did you get here?"

"Raoul brought me," she told him quickly, then paused at the concern that crossed his face.

"It's all right. I had to find you. We'll be out of here soon—don't worry."

"You shouldn't have come," her father whispered.

His mind must be wandering. Ana touched his forehead gently; he felt hot. They must get him to a hospital right away.

She turned to speak to the guard and saw a more familiar face enter the hut. "Raoul!" she cried. "Why didn't you tell me my father had been found? There's something else, too. I saw a man nearby—he attacked me a few days ago at the airfield. He's dangerous!"

Astonishingly, Raoul seemed unperturbed, patting his forehead with a spotless linen handkerchief. "Do not distress yourself; I have everything under control." He spoke to the guard at the door, his voice low.

Her father was stirring. Ana turned back to him, took his hand, trying to understand what he mumbled. "What is it, Dad?"

Then she saw traces of blood on his shirt, and she parted the stained fabric to see how badly he was hurt.

Her eyes widening, Ana stared at the angry-looking wound in his side. Even to her untrained eyes she could tell it was from a bullet.

She turned to Raoul. "He's been shot! How did he get this wound?" Ana stood up slowly, feeling the need to look Raoul in the eye; she was almost as tall as he.

"Yes." Raoul stood over her, his linen trousers only slightly creased as he returned the handkerchief to his pocket. "There were hostile tribes in the area, very unfortunate. His men were lucky to get him out when they did."

Ana shook her head. "I've seen some of the native tribes, Raoul. They carry bows and arrows, not guns. This is a gunshot wound. I'm not a child—now, tell me the truth! Who shot my father?"

"Very well." Raoul smiled pleasantly at her. "I did."

Fourteen

Ana stared at him, not believing her ears. "*You* shot my father? Why?"

"He was snooping where he had no business," Raoul said, as matter-of-factly as if he were discussing the current profit-and-loss statements. "It was unfortunate. So he had to be detained until I could make some changes."

"But you can't get away with this," Ana protested, trying to keep her voice from wavering. She felt dizzy, off-balance, almost as if the whole world had tilted beneath her feet.

"Why not?" Raoul asked, his tone suddenly fierce. "I did try to keep you from coming, but you wouldn't listen. You're much too headstrong, lovely Ana. My men had to smash the radio at the airfield because of you—such a nuisance. You forced me to instruct my men to follow you in your tiresome trek through the jungle, moving a body so the rude American boy wouldn't see it also and spread the news at his mother's camp. You've cost me one man already and much time and inconvenience. Now that you have seen, you must remain my guest for a while, also."

"And what will you do with us?" Ana demanded, then wished she hadn't asked. She had never seen Raoul's eyes look so cold.

"That remains to be seen. For the moment, you wanted to see your father; now you have your wish. You may tend to him and stay out of trouble. I have work to do." Raoul left the hut, while Ana searched futilely for some threat that would change Raoul's mind.

She could think of none.

Then her father spoke softly, and she dropped to her knees again to lean over him.

". . . shouldn't have come," he was telling her.

"I know, but I had to find out what had happened to you," Ana told him. "I was worried about you, Dad. What brought you here? You promised to meet me at the airport. Did you forget?"

Even in the midst of danger and deceit, it still mattered to her if he had meant what he said in his last letter, Ana realized.

Her father's smile was rueful. "Nothing could

have kept me away, dearest Ana. Except this." Weakly he gestured to his gunshot wound. "I did not forget you, nor did I mean to go away on business. The plane was supposed to take me only for an hour's flight. I would have been back well in time. But the pilot was in Raoul's pay. His men tied me up, brought me out here. And when I wouldn't cooperate, they shot poor Paolo, one of my most trusted men, right in front of my eyes, then wounded me."

She nodded in understanding. "At least I've found you. Dad, your letter—it meant so much to me. I'm so glad I have a chance to tell you that. Thank you for writing it."

He took her hand, though his grip was weak. "Dear little Ana, I'm truly sorry for the time I lost with you. I know my neglect is hard to forgive. I have so much to make up to you, and now I may not get the chance."

The weakness in his voice increased her fears. "Don't say that. We're going to get out of here. We're going to have that time together, Dad, lots of it."

Her father smiled, and Ana felt the old hurts, the old loneliness deep inside her, begin to heal. Her father did care for her; he had meant every word of the letter.

"I love you, little Ana," he whispered.

"I love you, too," she answered, leaning to kiss his cheek. She sat down beside him, still holding his hand as if she were afraid to let go.

For a few minutes they were silent, while Ana relished the miracle of her father alive and beside her. But she couldn't forget the rest of their reality, either; they were prisoners, lost in a massive jungle. With Raoul a ruthless captor, how would they ever get out alive?

"Did you know Raoul was dishonest, Dad?"

Her father shook his head, even the slight effort making him tremble. "I've been searching for someone behind a massive computer fraud," he told her, his voice very faint. "He hid his trail well at the company, but I found expenditures that couldn't be explained, money disappearing, too many puzzles. Now I know he's the one who has been forging my name to direct secret projects."

Ana nodded, remembering the map they had found at the first camp. "Brad thought it might be a gold mine," she told her father.

"Brad?"

"A friend of mine. It's a long story." Ana touched her father's forehead, worrying about the heat that flushed his skin. "Is there a doctor here? Has anyone done anything for your wound?"

"No." He was obviously in pain.

Ana bit her lip, wanting to scream at the

cruelty of the men who had treated her father like this, so that he might now lose his life through lack of care. He could die from loss of blood, from infection, from any of the many tropical diseases.

Worst of all, no one knew they were here, a prisoner of the man who was supposed to be one of her father's trusted aides.

But that wasn't true, Ana thought, hope returning with a rush. She sat up straighter. Emily Eliot had asked her to radio when she found her father. If she didn't call, they would wonder what had happened, maybe contact the authorities.

Then her spirits fell once again. How would anyone ever find them amid miles and miles of uncharted forest? Her father could die, and Ana, too, before help ever reached them.

But if Brad knew she was missing, he wouldn't sit back and do nothing. Brad knew the local jungle, knew many of the tribes. He'd know how to look for her. Would he?

She could almost see Brad's frown as she had flown off in the chopper with Raoul. How angry was he? How long until he cooled off, decided she might be in trouble? There was so much forest out there; even if he searched, how long would it take to find them?

She had to keep her father alive. Why hadn't Raoul killed him right away, now that the elder

Puentes knew Raoul's secret? Maybe it was a precaution, in case anyone questioned Raoul's forged signatures, or his orders at the home office. But he'd never let his boss leave alive, knowing all this. And the same fate must await Ana. She also knew too much.

"Oh, Brad," Ana murmured. "I hope you come. Hurry, I need you."

A tin basin of murky water lay near the hammock, and Ana bathed her father's face and some of his chest with her bandanna, the one Brad had given her. "Are you in much pain?"

"The greatest pain I feel now is regret that I brought you into this danger, Ana," her father told her quietly. "It's my fault you're here."

"You didn't tell me to rush off into the jungle," Ana said as cheerfully as she could.

"You may be impetuous, but you are also very brave," her father said, with a touch of his usual spirit. "We must find a way to get you out of here. You must not suffer because I have been blind. Raoul will not let me live now; I know it. I'm sorry you're here, little Anita," her father told her quietly. "Yet I'm also glad to see you once more before I die."

"Hush," Ana told him. "You're not going to die. I won't let you."

Jose Puentes stared back at her, his expression

sober. "Raoul is a devil; I never suspected he could be plotting so much. I know I can't escape, but we must think of a way to get you out of here."

"I'm staying right here with you," Ana told him firmly.

"There's so much I wish I could do over, change," her father said. "I've been dreaming a little while I lay in this hut. I remembered all the hours I spent at the office, and how seldom I took time for my family. The divorce was my fault, too; no wonder Alana finally left. How I wish I could go back and do it over again. But I can't undo the past."

Ana felt a surge of remembered anger, resentment she had nourished for years. "I wish you'd thought of it earlier, Dad," she told him softly.

"So do I, my dear."

The contrition in his voice was genuine. Ana felt a lump in her throat. If Raoul took away their future now, it would be unbelievably bitter. There would be no new beginning, no chance for a better relationship between them.

"I thought of you as a little girl, how precious you were to me. I don't think I've told you that. And now you're a young lady, and I don't even know you. I'm sorry I won't have the opportunity to make it up to you."

"Oh, Dad. I love you very much, no matter

what happens." Ana gripped his hand tightly.

"I love you, too. You are the best part of me, little Anita," her father told her.

The sound of someone entering the hut made Ana tense. It was Raoul.

"My father needs a doctor." Ana jumped to her feet. "I demand that you get him medical help! You can't expect to keep us here forever."

"Not forever, lovely Ana, just until I am ready to take over the company. Then no one will wonder that Jose Puentes has disappeared, humiliated and outmaneuvered. Now I have business to take care of, but I'll be back in a couple of days." His smile was as suave as ever.

So Raoul was leaving. Ana's mind started working feverishly. Was there any way she could turn his absence to their advantage?

"And I have radioed a message from you to your kind hosts, the mad botanist lady and her rude son. I told them you had found your father and were taking him back to the city for medical attention."

"What?" Ana knew that her expression reflected her dismay.

"Oh, yes. Did you think I would forget that they asked for a response? I always cover my tracks, lovely Ana. That's why I've succeeded this long. Until I return, *adeus*." With an ironic wave, Raoul left the hut.

Ana sat down by her father, feeling completely alone. Brad would think she had forgotten him, and he would have no reason to look for her. There was no hope of any help.

Her father had shut his eyes; his flushed face made her heart turn over. She wouldn't sit here and do nothing while Raoul plotted how best to kill them without exciting suspicion.

"Is there any water?" her father murmured.

Ana looked beside the hammock, but the plastic water bottle was empty. She went to the hut and pushed tentatively on the door. To her surprise, it opened easily under her touch.

Then she saw the big man, who jumped to his feet when she appeared in the doorway. Ana refused to show her fear.

"We need water—*água*." She showed him the empty water bottle.

Shrugging, he took the bottle, then motioned for her to return to the hut.

Ana went back inside, wondering if she had a chance to slip away while he went for the water. But she couldn't leave her father so ill, and she didn't know where to go for help, anyhow. She'd just get lost in the jungle again.

In a few minutes, the surly man returned. To Ana's dismay, he gave her the same bottle back, half-filled with murky water.

"No! We don't want water from the river. We need mineral water, *água mineral*. Raoul wants to keep my father alive. Please get me some bottled water!"

The man left again, and this time when he returned, he came into the hut carrying a heavy cardboard carton. When he dumped it into the dirt, Ana saw half a dozen sealed bottles of mineral water and nodded approval.

"Yes, that's right."

Their unwilling protector had also brought some canned food, and Ana remembered that she had a can opener in her backpack. She wasn't sure if her father would be able to eat, but she would try.

When she opened her pack, she came across some of Brad's supplies. The alcohol wipes were there—maybe she could clean her father's wound. Joy flooded through her when her hand brushed against a pill bottle. Antibiotics! *Thank you again, Brad. You help me even when you're not here.*

Feeling as though she'd found the gold the villains were no doubt in pursuit of, she knelt beside her father's hammock. "I'm going to see what your wound looks like, Dad. I have alcohol; maybe I can dress it a little better."

With a gray face, he nodded. Ana pulled aside the shirt, which had stuck to his skin with dried

198

blood, and began to probe gently around the shattered skin. She did what she could, worrying about the redness and swollen areas around the bullet wound—infection was already setting in. Eventually she got to his back. There was another wound! The bullet seemed to have gone straight through.

If no bullet had lodged inside, maybe her dad had hope, Ana thought, wishing she knew more about medicine. Biting her lip as she concentrated, Ana cleaned the two wounds as thoroughly as she dared, trying not to see her father's discomfort as he gritted his teeth against the pain. After flushing the wounds with bottled water, she packed them with alcohol wipes. Then, using her T-shirt as a bandage, she ripped his bloodstained shirt to tie the packing as securely as she could. Finally she gave her father two antibiotic tablets and bottled water to drink.

"You're not allergic to penicillin, are you, Dad?" she asked him.

He shook his head. "No. Where did you get the medicine, Ana?"

"It's a long story. I'll explain later," she told him. "I just hope this helps." Looking up, she saw that her father was watching her, an expression on his face she couldn't identify. Turning away, she busied herself with opening a can of soup.

"I know I'm improvising, Dad. I wish we could get you to a hospital. I wouldn't take chances with your health if I had a better choice." She helped him drink the thick broth.

He nodded. "I'm only admiring your courage; my little girl has truly grown up."

She hugged him gently, careful not to disturb the wound. "Whatever happens," she told him, "I'm glad I found you."

The hours seemed long until darkness fell. At dusk the surly guide tossed a hammock inside for Ana to string up. She and her father talked occasionally, and sometimes the elder Puentes slept, while Ana sat on the side of her hammock and thought about possibilities.

The night was long too, but Ana slept a little, and no one in the camp bothered them. Raoul must have left strict orders, Ana thought, grateful to him for that much as she remembered the leering menace of the tattooed man at the airfield.

The next morning, reminded of that incident, she asked her father, "Do you know anyone named Manuel?"

"Manuel Siventes?" her father asked.

"Could be. Who is he?"

"One of my vice presidents; when I first began to suspect that something was wrong in the company, I asked Manuel to do some checking."

Ana nodded as she spooned out some canned fruit for her father to eat. That explained the men's questions at the airfield.

"How do you feel this morning?"

"Not so bad," her father told her.

Ana suspected that was an understatement, but she gave him more antibiotic tablets and also shared her malaria pills. Then she went back to her plotting. Raoul would be back soon, and if she sat in this hut and waited for him, they would be like lambs waiting in their pen for the butcher to come. Yet her father was still much too weak to attempt a run through the jungle.

At the main camp, she had seen a hut with an antenna. If she could find a way to get to the radio inside, was there any way she could signal Brad?

"Good idea," Ana murmured to herself. "I know Brad's frequency. If I can remember how he worked the radio, and if I knew where the heck we were."

Ana knew that Raoul might overhear her call for help; he had the last time.

But she had to do something!

Fifteen

Ana woke before dawn, finding herself almost out of the hammock. In her dream, she had been wrestling with Raoul, but Raoul had tied her up with his silk tie, and Ana could only shout at him uselessly. Even in her dreams she couldn't escape.

Sitting here waiting for Raoul to decide how and when to finish them off was intolerable. Slipping out of her hammock, she looked around. The darkness seemed less intense. Her movement roused her father; he smiled wanly at her as Ana gave him water, then fed him canned soup and another antibiotic tablet, as well as his malaria pills.

Then she walked up and down the small hut, inspecting it more closely. Lifting the piece of canvas that hung over the one window, she saw that the opening was covered by two heavy pieces of wood, nailed firmly into the frame. But the hut itself was poorly constructed of thin wood and thatch. She could probably break through. But would the guards hear her efforts?

She began to test sections of the hut. One corner gave a little when Ana pushed against it; perhaps termites had weakened the wood, or carpenter ants.

Yet Ana hesitated, looking at her father. He was too weak to run. If she got away, would they take it out on her father?

Frowning, Ana considered. No, her father was the more important prisoner of the two. Until Raoul had his plans firmly in place, he needed the elder Puentes as insurance. When Raoul thought he could do without them, they would both be killed.

Her father seemed to follow her thoughts. "Can you get out? Then you must go, Ana. If you can just get away—"

Her odds weren't good, Ana thought, remembering the mazelike jungle. But seizing even the remotest chance was better than sitting here waiting to be murdered.

"I'll come back for you—I promise," she whispered, kissing his forehead. His skin didn't feel so warm this morning. She put the bottle of antibiotic tablets in his shirt pocket and left a full water bottle within easy reach of his hammock.

"Just get yourself to safety and contact the police," her father said, with a hint of his old authority. "They can take action. Don't come back to this place."

Ana nodded. This was no time to argue, but her private resolution was firm. "I love you, Dad," she said.

Then she added bottles of water to her pack, set it close by, and proceeded to attack the wall of the hut. It was more resistant than she'd expected, and Ana wondered if she was really trapped.

Her father saw her straining with the boards and sat up stiffly from his hammock.

"No, Dad," Ana protested.

He waved away her protest. "I'm not dead yet," he said firmly. "And if I have anything to say about it, neither are you."

Ana grinned at the echo of her father's usual assertiveness. Raoul had miscalculated if he thought he could defeat the Puentes family so easily.

With her father's help, the wall yielded. The weakened wood splintered, and they soon had a hole big enough for Ana to slide through.

"God keep you safe," her dad said softly. "I will cover the hole as much as I can, to delay their noticing it. But go as quickly as you can."

Ana squeezed his hand, then wiggled through the opening, pulling her backpack behind her. She was free! But the light was growing; she had to get away before she was seen.

The thought of the radio was an irresistible lure. If only she could signal for help. Looking around, she saw no sign of guards. They must think one wounded man and a "city girl" weren't in any danger of escaping, she told herself. She'd show them.

Quickly, Ana decided to risk investigating the hut where the radio was kept. She checked again for any sign of Raoul's men; then, gathering her courage, she headed stealthily for the main camp. The forest was quiet, but when she neared the camp, Ana almost lost her nerve. She had to cross a bare stretch of ground, with no more trees to hide behind. What if someone saw her?

It was now or never. She ran. Her footsteps seemed loud in the silence, her heart beat as thunderous as a drumroll. Gasping, Ana pressed herself against the rough thatch, waiting to hear a call of alarm. But the clearing remained silent; only a bird shrieked from the jungle beyond, making her jump.

Inching closer, she could see the radio from the window. Was there any chance of trying to use it, or would she only cause her own rapid recapture?

She edged around the hut, heading for the door, all the while watching for movement in the clearing. The black sky had faded, lightening slowly to the pale, clear blue of a forest dawn. Still, she heard no sounds.

She had reached the door. Ana pulled on it gently, praying for no betraying creak. When it was half-open, she eased herself forward, tiptoeing across the threshold.

And froze with fear. At her feet, sprawled across the dirt floor of the hut, lay one of Raoul's men.

Ana couldn't move. She bit back the scream of alarm that had risen to her lips. For one terrible moment, she thought the man was staring straight at her.

Then she saw that his eyes were closed, and he breathed heavily. An empty liquor bottle lay in the dirt where he'd dropped it, close to the machete that everyone in the jungle carried.

Maybe this was why the camp was late rising. The men may have taken advantage of the boss's absence. Grimacing, Ana looked at the radio, so near and yet so far. But the man was directly in her path, and even as she weighed the risk of trying to step over him, he stirred slightly.

As he shifted position, a small pouch in his shirt pocket opened slightly, and one pebble rolled onto the dirt, stopping as it hit Ana's athletic shoe. Watching the man closely, Ana bent to pick it up and tucked it inside her own pocket. Then she lifted his abandoned machete, backed out of the hut, and carefully eased the door shut without a sound.

She'd risked capture long enough here; it couldn't be much longer before someone came to check on them and found that she was absent. Ana had to make time while she could; Raoul's radio was out of reach. The machete felt good in her grip; it gave her more confidence, even though she doubted that she could swing it in anger.

Looking around one more time to make sure no one watched, Ana ran for the shelter of the forest. The short dash seemed very long. Her heart pounding, she reached the dimness of the tall trees, then paused, trying to decide which direction to go.

If she went in circles again, Raoul's thugs would find her quickly. She had to do better this time.

Ana studied the tall trees all around her, draped with twisted lianas and dotted with fungi. After the sour odors of the garbage-littered camp, the musty smell of forest greenery was comforting. The natives found their way through the jungle, and so did Brad. She wished he were here to guide her.

But this time, she was on her own. Ana tried to look at the jungle with Brad's eyes. Which way?

A tall tree trunk caught her eye—there! She saw a slash mark on the trunk, marking a trail. Ana hurried forward. Yes, a few feet farther on, she found another.

There was no way of knowing whether the trail had been made by natives or by Raoul's men. Either way, she might meet someone she didn't want to see. But the alternative was to wander blindly. Ana decided she had to take the chance. Holding the machete firmly in one hand, she set off.

At midmorning she paused to drink some water and eat a granola bar from her backpack. Had they discovered her absence back at the camp? They must have, yet so far she'd heard no sound of pursuit; perhaps she had a wide enough lead. Just where she was going, Ana wasn't sure. She only hoped this trail led eventually to an outpost where she could communicate with the outside world. She had to bring help back to her father.

The jungle was hushed around her in the midday heat; Ana wiped her forehead and returned her water bottle to her pack. Shouldering the pack, she set off again, hiking steadily around tall trees cloaked in the green dimness of the rain forest.

Within another hour, she saw signs of a clearing. Slowing her pace, Ana approached cautiously, not sure what she would find.

The sight that met her eyes when she edged closer made her stare in surprise. In the middle of the lush forest, the earth itself seemed to have been assaulted. Ana could hardly believe what she saw. Not only had the trees been ripped away, but the ground had been thrust open in wide paths of destruction. She saw a rusty bulldozer and some small tin huts on the far side of the wasteland. Along the barren land, Ana could already see signs of erosion, as rainwater cut through the unprotected dirt and washed away heavy gullies.

Was this one of the gold mines that Brad had spoken of? If this was part of Raoul's illegal schemes, she'd find no help here.

The trail had led her only into more danger. Now what could she do?

Ana sighed and prepared to backtrack. Then a movement at the edge of her vision made her jump. An old man came out of the forest and stared at her in surprise.

"It's all right," Ana said quickly in Portuguese. "I'm a friend."

He didn't seem much of a threat himself, unless he shouted to alert more of Raoul's men.

"I'm leaving now," Ana said, trying once more to reassure him.

The old man hobbled forward, putting one hand to his ear. "Eh?" he mumbled. He peered at her as if not sure of her intention.

He was deaf, Ana realized, not sure if this was good or not. She smiled and waved, pulling out a food bar from her pack and offering it to him.

He stared, then accepted the bar. Ripping open the wrapping, the old man took a bite.

Hoping she'd calmed his suspicions, Ana edged backward, happy to reach the protective shade of the trees. She would have to look for another trail. For the first time, she felt almost safe within the rain forest.

But she had gone only a few feet when out of the green darkness a shadow appeared, then another, and another. Gasping as the forms materialized in front of her, Ana saw that they were natives, with longer hair than the Yanomami and the same lack of costume. But these Indians were unfamiliar to her; the markings on their face and body were different, and the expressions of the faces glaring at Ana were much more savage. It was the tall bows and long arrows pointed at her heart that made her fear most vivid.

"I'm—I'm not an enemy," Ana stuttered in Portuguese, holding out her empty hands. She

211

tried to remember the greeting Brad had used with the Yanomami, but though she tried to copy the strange-sounding phrases, the Indians' grimaces did not ease. This was likely a different tribe, probably speaking a different language. Ana felt drops of sweat roll down her back and dampen her forehead. If she died here, without reaching help, her father would die too, in Raoul's hands.

The Indian who seemed to be the leader pulled back his bowstring, and Ana held her breath, waiting for the arrow to fly.

Then a shot rang out.

Sixteen

Ana saw the Indian closest to her grimace in surprise. He turned, and his arrow flew with a faint whine past Ana's head.

More shots. One of the Indians fell, even as more arrows zipped past her. Ana whirled to see where the gunfire came from. To her consternation, instead of the allies she had somehow hoped for, she saw the big man from Raoul's camp with several of his gang, all heavily armed. For the moment they seemed preoccupied with the greater threat of the Indians. And the natives had likewise turned their attention to these new invaders.

Ana ran for her life. More gunfire rang out, echoing through the forest with a hollow sound. She heard a slight thud behind her but couldn't stop to investigate. Sprinting across the leaf-covered ground, she tried to put as much distance between her and the two warring groups as she could, before someone had the leisure to notice her absence.

Ana ran around tall trees, dodging here and there, all thought of the trail lost. All she wanted now was to get as far from the conflict as she could. But as she ran on, the dim light deceived her, and she stumbled over a protruding tree root, falling heavily to the ground.

Grunting from the impact, she sat up quickly. After scrambling to her feet, she brushed off the dead leaves and debris. Then she picked up the machete—she had almost forgotten it was still clutched in her hand until she dropped it in the fall.

With a shock, she saw that a long arrow stuck out from her backpack. A trickle of water showed that a plastic bottle had been hit. It could have been her. Shivering, Ana tried to pull out the arrow, but it was firmly lodged. Her fall had splintered the shaft; she broke the long end off so that it wouldn't catch in a liana and trip her up, but the arrowhead and almost a foot of shaft remained. She had no time to worry about it now; there were more natives in the jungle, and some might be following her.

There was a terrible stitch in her side from running, and her breath came in labored gasps.

But it was impossible to stop even for a moment's rest. Raoul's men would simply take her back to camp, and what the Indians intended to do with her, she didn't even want to know. Her pace had slowed, but she pounded heavily on, stubbornly refusing to give up.

At last the pain in her side made running physically impossible. Ana paused behind a thick tree, bending almost double as she fought to catch her breath. Gasping for air, she hugged her aching sides. Had she lost them? Was it possible that she'd really given them the slip?

No, Ana could hear a suspicious rustling. How far away? It probably wasn't an animal; any forest creatures would have been frightened into flight by the noise of the battle.

It didn't sound like a native, either—they traveled through the jungle more quietly. This must be one of Raoul's men, and Ana feared them more than the Indians.

Struggling to her feet, Ana set out again. She was still too exhausted to make rapid progress, but every foot between her and her pursuers could only improve her chances. She was too weary to run, but she moved as quickly and silently as she could.

Of course, she had no idea in which direction she was heading, and she'd lost sight of the path long ago. Ana only prayed she wasn't traveling in circles, to end up at the mine, where more of the gang might be waiting.

But right now, she was mainly worried about the man or men who followed her. Ana made her way through the jungle as quietly as she could, trying to remember how Brad and his Yanomami friends had traveled so lightly over the forest floor. Yet every time she thought she might have lost her pursuer, a rustle of leaves behind her sent her pulse leaping, and she struggled on. The ground beneath her feet was becoming marshy and damp; was she coming to another river? Ana hoped she wouldn't be trapped by the stream. Could she change direction?

But as she tried to edge another way, the sounds seemed closer. Ana hurried on, fear rippling through her whole body like a cold current.

Her side ached again, but she was too frightened to stop. Panting, she loped on through the trees, making less effort to walk silently. Her attempt to disappear into the forest hadn't worked. All she could do now was flee.

She passed still more trees; then, with an abruptness that made her catch her breath, Ana found herself on the bank of a sluggishly flowing river. She almost walked straight into the dark, murky water but caught herself in time and jumped back. The bank was muddy and slick. Grasping a young seedling, she pulled herself along the bank, looking for firmer ground, for a better place to hide from whoever tracked her.

But it was too late. A man emerged from the trees, shouting in triumph when he saw her. It was the big man from the radio hut, the one from whom she had taken the machete.

Another man came out several yards lower down and headed toward her. Meanwhile, the big man was closing in.

Ana lifted her stolen machete, determined not to give in meekly.

But this man had armed himself with another machete, besides the pistol now tucked into his belt. As soon as he was close enough to be heard, he thrust out his empty hand.

"Where is it?" he demanded in hoarse Portuguese. "Give back what you stole!"

What—the machete? Ana blinked at him in surprise. Why on earth would he be concerned over one rusty blade? But she held on to it grimly; it was the only weapon she had.

He moved forward again, reaching for her. Ana stepped backward and almost slipped into the river. Reaching for a midsized tree that was closest to her, she pulled herself back.

The trunk felt reasonably smooth against her

palm, and it gave her a sudden, desperate idea. Without taking her eyes off the big man, and praying for no ants or wicked thorns, she turned and scrambled quickly up the tree.

The man yelled at her. "Stop!"

Ana ignored his angry shouts, scrabbling up the tree about fifteen feet to a limb that seemed large enough to bear her weight. Then she edged out to straddle the branch, clinging to it tightly.

The man in the rear laughed, and the big man glared at him. He pulled the pistol from his belt and pointed it at her.

Ana felt as cornered as a squirrel with hunters all around, but she forced herself to speak calmly. "If you shoot me, I'll fall into the river, and you'll never get back what you want."

The big man hesitated, growled something obscene, then put his gun back into his belt. He gripped his machete instead and jumped closer to the tree, motioning to the man behind him. "Come on!"

But in his haste, he misjudged the angle of the muddy bank. Slipping, he couldn't regain his balance and, with a splash, toppled headfirst into the water. He sat up choking and spitting, swearing briskly in Portuguese.

Ana held on to her branch, watching as her

erstwhile attacker yelled to his comrade to pull him out.

The smaller man was laughing, but he waded out toward the big guy, ready to pull him back to dry land.

Then the big man screamed. He lurched forward, trying to get to his feet, then fell again.

Watching with widened eyes, Ana gasped as she saw blood flow from a large gash in the man's arm.

The big man couldn't seem to make it to his feet. He thrashed and yelled for help, but his companion, pale with terror, turned instead and splashed noisily back toward the bank.

Piranhas!

Ana felt sick. She could hear wild splashes and groans as the struggle continued, the water now dark with blood. More of the small, deadly fish swam to attack; she could see the water rolling with movement just beneath the surface. Soon the big man slid farther under, his eyes dazed, his shouts fading to incoherent gasps.

There was no way she could help. Ana clutched her tree limb with renewed urgency, unable to watch.

The second man clambered back onto the muddy ground. He emerged from the water with several slashes on his legs bleeding freely. He stared at the water for a moment, then shuddered and turned away. Seeming to have lost all interest in Ana, he turned and limped through the trees, back the way he had come.

The big man's body had disappeared completely beneath the water, though she still could see frantic movements of the feeding fish. Ana trembled so hard she thought she might fall, and she clung even tighter to her branch.

Then she heard an ominous creak. Looking over, Ana thought her heart might stop. Her weight was too much for the slender branch; she saw a crack appear where it joined the main trunk. Afraid to move, Ana held her breath. If the branch broke, she would be tossed into the deadly waters of the river, and the piranhas would have two treats that day.

Time seemed to stand still. Only the river moved with its murderous inhabitants. The crack—was it growing larger?

There was no one here to help. Sitting frozen with fear until the limb finally broke would accomplish nothing. Yet if she moved, would it only make the limb break faster? She had to take the chance. She threw the machete toward the ground and watched helplessly as it plopped into the river. Then she eased slowly out of her pack and swung it farther inland, with better results.

Relieved of a little weight, the branch trembled but held steady. Now Ana slid as lightly as she could back toward the trunk.

The branch creaked in protest, and she lunged forward, grabbing the trunk as the branch tilted toward the river. Holding to the tree trunk, Ana slid much too fast down the almost-smooth bark. She felt pain in her palms and her thighs, but the alternative was unthinkable.

She hit the muddy ground with a thud, holding on to the tree for dear life. Her hands and legs were scraped and no doubt bleeding, but she could attend to them later. A centipede dropped onto her bare arm; Ana gasped but managed to maintain her grip. The creature crawled with its many legs over her arm, then dropped harmlessly to the ground. Sighing, Ana used the trunk to steady herself as she circled until she was on the side away from the river. Holding the trunk, she was able to reach her backpack.

Finally she could let go of the tree and step back. Avoiding another taller tree heavily draped with lianas, she knelt on the fallen leaves beneath, regardless of any scurrying insects. To be so close to an awful death—she still felt weak.

In a few minutes, using her hands gingerly, she opened her pack, careful not to touch the arrowhead. She found an alcohol wipe to clean some of the dirt from her bleeding palms and her scraped legs, then gulped down some water from the only bottle still intact. Next she used her nail scissors to split her bandanna in two and wrap it around her damaged hands.

She had to face the jungle again, and this time, she didn't know where to go. But returning to the mine site was useless, even if she could locate it after her wild rush through the forest. Ana felt her spirits sink even lower. Her father was waiting, still a prisoner in Raoul's camp. She had to try.

Just as Ana reached for her pack to put away the water, the jungle itself seemed to attack her. A thick strand of liana suddenly slid away from the tree trunk and dropped around her neck. Before she could react, another coil tightened around her chest.

Stunned, Ana stared down into the cold eyes of an anaconda.

Seventeen

Ana tried to scream but couldn't get her breath. This must be a bad dream—the giant snake was the stuff nightmares were made of. But the deadly pressure around her chest was no illusion. Uselessly she struggled against the smooth coils with their mottled pattern of brown, tan, and gold, trying to push them away, to somehow disentangle herself from the snake's grasp.

But she could barely move her arms; the anaconda was too strong. Even as Ana strove to push one section of the long body away, another tightened around her chest. She couldn't breathe; her vision darkened; blackness danced in front of her eyes. This was the end—not just for her, but for her father, too.

"Fight, Ana!" someone shouted. "Don't give up."

She couldn't see, couldn't take a breath. But

she felt the suffocating grip of the great snake loosen slightly as another pair of strong hands pulled at its coils. The blackness receded.

Brad! With new hope, Ana pushed at the constricting bands that threatened her life.

The snake, forced to confront a new enemy, opened its jaws, darting with surprising speed toward Brad.

Brad grabbed the head, gripping it so the jaws couldn't open to grab on to his arm. "Get out when I twist," he told Ana. "Now!"

With Brad throwing all his weight against the snake, Ana slid out of the anaconda's encircling coils. Falling limply onto the ground, she gasped for air. Taking long, shuddering breaths, she willed the forest to stop spinning around her.

But when her vision cleared, what she saw made her cry out. Brad was losing his struggle with the boa. Unable to let go of the head, he couldn't control the long body that inexorably wrapped itself around him, one loop at a time.

Knowing how quickly the anaconda could lock itself on to his chest, suffocating its newest victim, Ana looked around wildly for a weapon. If only she hadn't lost her machete. Brad's machete was tucked into his belt, beneath the snake and out of her reach. Grabbing a fallen branch, she hit the snake as hard as she could.

The tree limb broke uselessly in two.

"Oh, help," Ana muttered. Would Brad die because he'd come to her aid? She had to do something!

The broken shaft of the Indian arrow, still imbedded in her backpack, caught her eye. Ana grabbed the fragment of shaft and pulled. This time, desperation gave her new strength. She pulled it free, falling back on her heels as it came loose from her pack.

Holding the arrow by the broken shaft, she attacked the snake with the arrowhead. If only she could do enough damage to make the snake release its grip on Brad, but was the pointed bamboo head lethal enough? Again and again, Ana struck the snake's thick body, piercing the smooth scales with the sharp arrowhead.

Still Brad struggled, though his face darkened as he fought to breathe.

But Ana's repeated jabs seemed to have some effect. The snake moved more sluggishly, and the coils gripping Brad's chest and arms loosened.

"Keep it up," Brad whispered, gasping for air.

Ana redoubled her efforts, and the snake's strength seemed to fade. Brad pushed the heavy loops away and struggled out of the snake's encircling hold.

The snake lay still, stretched across the forest

floor. Ana looked at it in astonishment; the small arrowhead had done this?

But Brad was free—she grabbed him, hugging him wildly. "Oh, Brad, I thought I'd never see you again. I'm so glad you came. My father's been shot. It was Raoul—you were right, I should have listened—I'm always rushing off—but we have to save him—"

"Hold on," Brad protested; then he bent to meet her lips. The kiss was long and hard, and Ana felt the excitement tingle through every inch of her body. This time she could fully return Brad's passion, holding nothing back. His grip on her arms tightened, and they kissed until they were breathless. When they finally fell apart, Ana laid her head on Brad's shoulder, still savoring his touch. "It's good to see you again," he whispered against her hair.

"And you, too. But look at this snake. Is it dead?"

"Maybe—depending on the arrow poison," Brad explained, getting slowly to his feet.

Poison? She'd heard about natives using poisoned arrows, but somehow she hadn't thought of it when she'd been trying to pull it out earlier. And just as well. Ana shuddered. "Is it curete?"

"Could be. There are several types. But the important thing is that it at least paralyzed the snake. I don't know if the poison is strong enough to kill it; let's get out of here just in case it comes around."

Nodding, Ana picked up her pack and offered Brad an arm to lean on.

He looked a little wobbly, but his pace picked up as they made their way from the scene of the struggle. "They don't usually attack people," Brad told her. "How'd you get so lucky?"

"I don't know. I was kneeling on the ground."

"Probably looked about dinner size to the anaconda," Brad told her.

Ana shuddered. "Not funny. How did you find me?" She had been too preoccupied with the immediate threat to wonder about his miraculous appearance.

"I had the map, remember, that I took from the Puentes camp. The mine's location was marked, and I thought it was a good place to start looking for you. When I saw the goons with the guns, I was trying to decide what to do. Then the Indians arrived. I slipped around the fight and followed you when you ran, but I lost you in the forest."

"Thank God you finally came," Ana murmured. "You saved my life—again."

"And you returned the favor." Brad's blue eyes twinkled.

Ana looked at the smooth curve of his lips and wished she had time to stop and thank him properly. But this was hardly the time or the place. "But why did you come at all?"

227

"You didn't radio us, and you promised Mom you would. I didn't think you would have forgotten."

"Raoul told me that he sent a message in my name," Ana said.

Brad grimaced. "I wouldn't believe that sleaze-ball; I didn't trust him from the beginning. I told you not to go off with him."

"You were right about him," Ana agreed. "But oh, Brad, I was right about my dad. My father isn't behind the illegal mining—and I'm so relieved. I just knew he couldn't be a criminal. It was Raoul all the time, using the Puentes name. I'd like to string him up for that alone. He kidnapped my father, shot him, and held him captive. I have to go back for my dad. Raoul will kill him for sure."

She stopped, turning to meet Brad's gaze squarely in the green dimness. "Can you help me get back to the camp? If we circle the mine, I think we can find the trail."

Brad frowned. "Ana, that won't work. We should go back to my mom's camp and radio for help. What can we do against a well-armed gang?"

"There isn't time," Ana argued. "When Raoul thinks he's secure, he's going to murder my father. I can't risk it." Ana heard the urgency in her own voice and hoped Brad believed her.

"This is crazy." Brad shook his head.

"Maybe." Her hands, already raw after her hasty

descent down the tree, bled anew from her struggle with the giant snake. Her chest ached from the anaconda's pressure, and she felt tired and afraid. But she'd never forgive herself if she gave up now and trooped back to safety, leaving her father to be murdered in the middle of the jungle.

Taking a deep breath, Ana made up her mind. "You go back and radio for help. I'm heading for the camp."

"Ana, don't be stupid. You can't even find the trail unless I show you the way." Brad's frown deepened.

"I have to try." Feeling very much alone, Ana trudged away from him, leaving him behind yet again. Was this to be the pattern of their relationship?

Brad ran to catch up. "You're going the wrong way."

She shook her head. "I told you—"

"And I'm telling you, that's not the way to the mine."

"You mean you'll come?" Renewed hope made even the green dimness of the forest seem lighter. Ana gave Brad an impulsive hug. "Oh, thank you!"

"I should have my head examined," Brad told her grimly, pointing the way. "And I will, if I have any head left to examine by the time this is over."

His crack reminded her unpleasantly of the

hostile tribe she had encountered at the mine site. Glancing around nervously, Ana lowered her voice. "Who are the natives who tried to kill me?"

Brad shrugged. "I'm not sure. But they looked as if they meant business. Some of them carried dart guns; they may be a tribe from farther west, maybe the foothills."

"Why were they out to get me?"

"Probably figured you're one of the miners. Or they're just mad at any intruder—who knows?" Brad told her. "You were lucky to get away. Those guys can be pretty single-minded."

Ana bit her lip at the memory. "I could tell. Worse than that, two of Raoul's men followed me like bloodhounds. I took a machete from one of the gang back at their camp, and he wanted it back; I don't know why."

Brad raised his dark brows. "He followed you through the jungle for a lousy machete? Are you sure?"

"That's what he said—at least—" A sudden thought struck her. "Oh, Brad, that's not all I took from the camp. When I tried to get to the radio, a drunk guy was blocking the way. When he shifted, a rock rolled out of his pocket and I picked it up."

Now she fished the small pebble from her pocket and showed it to Brad. Some of the mud had flaked off in her pocket, and she saw that it had a quartzlike consistency.

Brad whistled softly. "No wonder they want to keep this discovery secret. I thought it didn't look much like a gold mine."

"You mean it's not gold?" Ana stared at him.

Brad's blue eyes were solemn. "That's a rough-cut diamond."

Ana gasped. She examined the rough piece of stone again; it no longer looked so small. "It must be five or six carats, at least!"

Brad nodded. "I guess. Hard to tell until it's cut properly. But Amazonian diamonds are of excellent quality, I've heard. Your friend Raoul must be getting rich."

"And destroying the rain forest to get it," Ana added, frowning. "As well as my father's good name."

"Too bad we couldn't bring the anaconda with us." Brad looked grim. "Here's a tree slash; I think this is your trail."

Ana put the diamond back in her pocket. "This could be it, although all the trees look pretty much alike."

"I know the mine is that way." Brad pointed. "So if we backtrack, we should find the camp where your father's being held. Just what do you expect to do when we get there?"

Ana hated to admit that she didn't have a clue. "I'll think of something."

"They're not just going to hand over your

father when you ask nicely," Brad said, and once again Ana gritted her teeth at his habit of announcing the obvious.

"No, duh. Brad, I said you didn't have to come. But I can't just stand back and wait for my father to be killed. What if it were your mother?"

"Point taken." Brad's tone was rueful. "Okay, count me in."

Ana had a crazy desire to laugh. Two people with no weapons to speak of against a well-armed and determined criminal syndicate. The odds were stacked so high against them, she didn't even want to think about it. Still, with Brad beside her, nothing seemed impossible.

They reached Raoul's camp just before dark and watched for activity from a safe distance. Ana saw two men who looked familiar, the short guy with the mustache and another who had donned a wool poncho as the temperature dropped.

The hut where her father was being kept still had a guard beside it. Thank goodness, she told herself. At least that meant he was still alive. Ana was happy to see no sign of Raoul. Not only did that mean one less jerk to deal with, but Ana suspected that the rest of the men would be less alert without the boss around.

While she and Brad crouched behind a tree

trunk, she whispered, "If we set a hut on fire, would it burn down the whole forest?"

Brad shook his head. "Not likely. It's pretty damp here, you know, so it would take some effort to burn a rain forest. But what good would setting a fire do? You'd have all the men out at once to put it out."

"I thought maybe we could distract them," Ana explained. "Get my father while they're all occupied and slip away."

"To where? Doesn't sound like your father's ready to hike through the jungle. And we don't have a boat."

Ana bit her lip. "Okay, got a better idea?"

"You said they have a radio. Wait till everyone's asleep. Then get to the radio and call for help."

"What if Raoul picks up the message?" Ana asked.

"Hope he doesn't, that's all."

Not exactly a perfect plan, but the best one they had. It seemed a long time till the last man disappeared into the huts. While they waited, they carefully went over different possible outcomes of their raid and talked about various plans they could use to cover most eventualities. Finally her father's guard checked on his prisoner one last time, then ambled off to his own hammock.

Mosquitoes swarmed in noisy clouds. Ana pulled the insect repellent out of her backpack and rubbed it generously over her exposed skin, offering the bottle to Brad. Hours passed, and still they waited. The jungle night was dark but not quiet; monkeys shrieked and swung in the treetops overhead, and other strange noises made Ana's heart beat fast. Brad picked up some of the muddy earth beneath them and rubbed his face and arms. Grimacing, Ana did the same. Camouflage.

Finally Brad whispered, "I think we can make a move."

This time, her heart seemed to gallop. But she said as calmly as possible, "I'm ready."

Moving quietly, they approached the camp. The clearing seemed much bigger to Ana when they had to leave the protection of the trees and cross to the radio hut.

"What if someone's in the hut?" she whispered to Brad.

"Go to Plan A, like we discussed," he mouthed back.

The door of the radio hut wasn't locked. Brad eased it open, then slid inside. Ana followed quickly. Brad stood very still just inside the door, his finger to his lips. Holding her breath, Ana looked around the room, just barely able to make out objects. Across the room, a hammock was strung from the walls of the hut, and a sagging figure snored softly.

Brad pointed, and Ana nodded. Plan A. She slipped behind the sleeping man and pulled a pair of socks out of her pack. Then she fished another of Brad's bandannas out of her shorts pocket. Brad walked quietly to the man's other side. Then he lifted a can of soup from a box on the floor and hit him on his head, hard.

The sleeper gave a startled grunt, but before he could call out, dazed and bewildered, Ana stuffed the socks into his mouth and tied them in place quickly with the bandanna.

Before the man knew what was happening, Brad had tied his hands and feet securely with rope from his backpack, leaving him swinging in the string hammock. When the prisoner tried to struggle, Brad held his machete in front of the stranger's face. The man's struggles subsided abruptly; he hung in his hammock, as helpless as a sausage in its casing.

Ana felt elated; maybe this would actually work.

Brad crossed to the radio, pulled a small flashlight from his pack, and shielding it with one hand, studied the controls.

Then he shut off the light and touched the knobs and dials. The sounds he made seemed very loud in the silence; Ana thought the whole camp must hear. Nervously she looked through the one window for signs of movement, but nothing in the camp stirred.

The radio crackled; Brad leaned forward and spoke as quietly as he could into the mike.

"Mayday, Mayday, this is an emergency," he said in Portuguese. "I need a helicopter to come to these coordinates with government troops. There is a wounded man being held prisoner, and an illegal mining operation run by armed criminals."

Would anyone hear? Ana felt her whole body tense as she waited for someone to respond. The minutes crawled by; how long had they been crouched here by the radio?

Over and over, Brad repeated his call, twisting the knobs and trying different frequencies. Still the radio gave them no response. Was no one listening at this time of night? What would they do next?

Then a bright light hit the hut, flashing through the window opening. The roar of a helicopter motor brought Ana's heart into her throat, and an explosion of bullets ripped through the thin walls of the hut.

Someone *had* heard their call. Raoul!

Eighteen

"Look out!" Ana called, as if Brad wouldn't notice the barrage of gunfire.

Brad crouched lower but continued to broadcast. "Anyone," he said in rapid Portuguese. "Anyone who hears, my location is—"

Ana dropped to the ground. Above her, the man they had tied in his hammock struggled frantically, obviously fearing the gunfire. Ana looked around wildly, saw his machete, and crawled to grab it. Risking a quick leap, she slashed the hammock strings, and the man fell heavily to the floor. His hands and feet were still tied, but he had as much protection as they did. Then Ana turned to watch Brad.

Brad shouted into the mike. "Mayday!"

A new round of gunfire blasted the radio, and

glass exploded through the hut. Ana covered her face with her hands, then looked up again, afraid of what she would see.

Brad lay slumped on the ground, his body covered with splinters of glass.

"Brad!"

Forgetting the continuing erratic blasts from Raoul's helicopter, Ana ran to Brad. He was unconscious. She brushed the glass off his back, looked for any wounds, then touched his chest to see if his heart was beating.

Yes, she could feel a steady rhythm, thank heavens. But there was a bump on his head, and blood flowed from his thigh; a bullet seemed to have grazed his leg. Ana tried to see how bad it was. Did Brad still have medical supplies inside his pack? Working quickly, she wrapped clean gauze around the wound to stanch the flow of blood.

As if it mattered. Raoul would kill them all as soon as he landed, and she could hear the chopper dropping closer to the clearing.

Outside the hut, men were shouting. Everyone in the camp must have been awakened by Raoul's gunfire, as well as the sounds of the chopper itself.

The chopper's engines changed as the aircraft touched down, then slowed its noisy clatter. Ana heard more voices, and, yes, that was Raoul, coming toward the radio hut.

"See if anyone's still alive," she heard him say in his usual arrogant tone. "Bring them out. I want to see for myself."

Brad was still unconscious. Ana crouched beside him, the machete useless now in her hand. There was no place to hide in the tiny hut, no way to surprise the approaching killer, no other way out. Trapped.

The door opened, and someone turned a flashlight in her direction. The strong beam caught Ana square in the face; instinctively she narrowed her eyes. A man walked across the hut and pulled her roughly to her feet, while another released the man who had been bound and gagged. Part of her wanted to cry out but wouldn't give Raoul the satisfaction.

The gang leader stood in the doorway, watching them. His dark eyes were hooded in the shadows cast by the chopper's bright lights; he looked like a demon. How had she ever thought him handsome?

"Is she alone? Ah, I see. Is he dead?" His tone was so casual.

The other man kicked Brad with his booted foot. Though Ana winced vicariously at the blow, Brad remained limp.

"Near enough. Bring her out." Raoul turned and walked back into the light from the helicopter.

The man pushed her forward. Staggering, Ana barely managed to stay erect. In a moment she found herself in the middle of the clearing, facing Raoul's cool survey. The whole camp was awake now, and half a dozen of Raoul's men stood watching, grinning as they waited for their boss to finish her off. Ana wondered if her father was awake in his hut, if he knew that she had come back for him, had tried at least to save him.

I love you, Dad, she thought. *I'm glad I had the chance to tell you that, and to know that you meant every word in your letter. You didn't let me down this time. I tried not to let you down, either. Sorry I didn't do a better job. If I'd had more time—*

Raoul wasn't going to give her any time. "Why did you come back?" he demanded. "You got away, then walked back into my arms. Why?"

"To save my father." She stood up as straight as she could.

"Such loyalty. It's a shame you're not on my side, pretty Ana, for more reasons than one, but I'm afraid I could never trust you. Still, you should have something for your trouble; you've cost me an expensive radio and much inconvenience. I don't like being annoyed, pretty Ana. Bring the old man," he told one of his henchmen. "She will see him die first. Then the daughter will follow the father."

"No!" Ana said, her voice wavering despite her best efforts. But no one listened. She had to wait numbly until two of Raoul's men brought her father, barely able to walk on his own, from his hut. They pushed him to stand beside her; Ana reached to take his hand.

Ana saw tears in her father's eyes. "I wish you had not come back, my dear," he told her quietly. "But it was very brave."

"I love you, Dad," Ana whispered.

"And I, you." He squeezed her hand.

"Touching." Raoul sounded bored. "I think we've had enough sentiment for one night. Let's end this; I need some sleep." He motioned to one of his men, standing ready with a long weapon.

Ana held her breath, bracing herself for the impact of the bullets, hoping it would be quick.

But a cry from one of his men made them all pause.

"Fire!"

Ana turned with the rest and saw flames shooting from the radio hut. She gasped. What about Brad?

Raoul shouted directions. "Get some water from the river! Put it out before it reaches the ammo!"

Men ran here and there; for an instant, Ana and her father seemed forgotten. She thought of running for the forest. She put one hand under her father's arm to support him; perhaps they could reach the darkness under the trees. He nodded, reading her intent, and she guided him toward the shadows. One foot, two.

"Not so fast, pretty Ana." Raoul gripped her shoulder. "You'll stay right here."

Ana shook her head in frustration, and her father leaned weakly against her.

There were shouts from the hut as the men fought the fire. One man approached them as they stood near the trees, the short man in the poncho. But he seemed to have grown taller.

"What do you want, Pedro? Help the others," Raoul told his man impatiently.

"I don't think so," Brad's voice said quietly. "Put the gun down, Raoul."

Ana's eyes widened; then she saw Brad's face beneath the grime, and the muzzle of a gun showing clearly beneath the enveloping poncho.

Raoul blinked in surprise, his handsome face looking annoyed.

"Drop it, now," Brad repeated. He lifted his gun.

Raoul moved quickly, his grip on Ana's shoulder painful as he pulled her in front of him. Ana struggled wildly, but Raoul had his arm around her throat, and the pressure made her gasp.

"Shoot!" she whispered. "I don't care."

Brad hesitated, his expression twisted.

"Ah, but *he* does," Raoul almost purred. "Drop the gun, or she will die."

I'll die anyhow, Ana thought, but she couldn't speak again; he was pressing so hard against her throat that consciousness was fading.

Dimly, she heard Brad say, "No!" and knew with a sinking heart that he had put down his gun.

Raoul released her, and she wavered, her knees weak. Brad, now a prisoner too, took a quick stride and grabbed her.

"Good try," she whispered.

"The fire was your idea." Brad put his arm around her, and she leaned against him; her father stood close on her other side. Raoul picked up the gun, and Ana thought fuzzily, *Maybe dying isn't too bad if you have people you love beside you.*

"You have caused me enough trouble," Raoul told them, pointing the gun at them.

Silently, Ana leaned against Brad and waited.

But Raoul's arm dropped, and when he pulled the trigger, the bullets flew uselessly into the dirt.

Was he taunting them?

Then Ana saw that Raoul's expression was strange. His eyes glazed; he toppled forward into the dirt. Two long arrow shafts protruded from his back.

While she stared in astonishment, Brad's grip on her shoulders tightened. "Stay very still," he murmured to her father. "Running won't do any good."

Running from what? Then Ana saw the dark shadows slipping out of the woods, holding bows and dart guns. The Indians who had raided the mining site were back.

For the first time, she realized that no one shouted from the other huts—no one moved except the dark figures of the natives. Were all of Raoul's men dead? Would they be next?

Ana blinked at the headman, who now stood in front of them. His face was painted black and his expression was hard to read.

Brad spoke quietly, but the chieftain's expression didn't change. Using a different dialect, Brad tried again, but there was still no response. Ana felt frozen; she could only wait and listen.

One more time Brad tried, and this time the chief blinked, then spoke gutturally and rapidly in response.

"He says, why shouldn't we also die? We have poisoned the land and ripped it apart," Brad translated in a murmur.

While he answered the chief, Ana whispered, "But it wasn't us!"

The headman didn't look convinced.

"Tell him we'll go away and never come back," Ana whispered to Brad.

He spoke, and the headman answered, his tone adamant. Behind the tribal leader, half a dozen Indians held bows with arrows ready. Poisoned arrows, Ana remembered from her attack on the anaconda. Had they escaped death at Raoul's hands only to find it in these natives?

An idea came to her. "Tell him," Ana told Brad, "we have the soul of the mine and he can destroy it, if he will just let us go."

"What do you mean?" Brad threw her a puzzled glance.

"Tell him!"

Brad translated, and the chief looked puzzled too. Moving very slowly, Ana slipped the pack off her back and opened it. She took out the folded map of the mine, with the photos glued to it, and held it out for the Indians to see.

"Tell him this is the soul of the mine that drew the strangers into their land. This is its name, its true name. We will destroy it, and no one else will know what it is or where to find it."

Brad translated. The headman watched her, his eyes bright in the glare of the fire still smoldering behind them, his expression suspicious.

Slowly Ana knelt, drew out a match, and lit the map in two places. For a moment it smoldered;

then the paper caught and the flame grew, flaring when it touched the photos.

They all watched the fire consume the large paper, and then, as it crumpled into black ash, Ana held her breath. Would the Indians kill them anyway?

The headman spoke.

"He says, what will stop us from coming back, or telling others?" Brad translated.

"Tell him the name is gone, and we will not know how to find this place again." Ana tried to make her voice sound sincere. Their lives depended on this. She drew a deep breath, met the chieftain's gaze squarely.

For a small eternity, they looked at each other. Then the Indian stepped back. While she watched, hardly believing, the Indians slipped into the trees, disappearing as rapidly as they had come.

Ana held her breath—had they done it? The clearing was silent. Relief washed through her like currents of electricity. She wasn't going to die, after all. Her father, Brad—they were all alive.

Brad looked at her, his grin a little crooked. "Ever think of a career in the diplomatic corps?"

Throwing herself into his arms, she kissed him wildly. Then she hugged her dad, then Brad again. Her soreness, her bruises, the cold dampness that made her shiver—none of it mattered. The first blush of dawn touched the night sky, easing the blackness. Raoul was dead, and the natives were gone. They were going to live.

Somehow her knees were very weak. "I think I have to sit down," she told them as her legs folded. "Brad, are we going to have to walk out of here? The radio's smashed."

"There's a radio in the chopper," Brad told her. "We'll arrange a rendezvous far enough away so that we don't run into the tribe again. We may have used up our quota of miracles."

Ana laughed, and the other two joined in. It didn't matter that their laughter wobbled. Daylight streaked the purple sky.

A week later Ana stepped down from another helicopter to the landing site at the Eliot camp. A smiling Brad reached up to help her. She jumped off the chopper step and into his arms.

"Oh, Brad, I've missed you!"

Brad's hug almost took her breath. "I thought you'd be at the hospital with your dad." They ducked under the chopper's rotors and headed for the shade of the nearest thatched shelter.

"He threw me out," Ana explained cheerfully. "He said if I fluffed the pillows one more time, the nurses would rebel, because I wasn't giving them enough to do."

Brad laughed and poured her some lemonade.

Ana accepted the tin mug, then recaptured his hand. He looked wonderful, his dark hair waving and unruly, his blue eyes sparkling—because she was here? Ana smiled to herself at the thought.

"He's improving every day, so I wasn't worried to leave him. Besides, now he's working with three assistants and two laptops trying to straighten out the mess that Raoul has made of the company, and the police need all the records, and—and, mostly, he'll always be a workaholic. That's just the way he is, and he'll probably never change.

"We've spent a lot of time talking, and I feel a lot closer to him. But I can't change his character, and I wouldn't want to. I'm proud of his drive and his determination."

Brad looked at her closely. "That sounds a lot like someone else I know. But he's going to spend more time with you?"

"Yeah. As soon as he's released from the hospital, we're going to have a real vacation. But in the meantime, your mom told me I could come and help out here."

"She did?" Brad lifted his brows in the familiar gesture. It didn't irritate Ana any longer. She reached out to touch his arched brows tenderly.

Brad took her hand, pressed it against his cheek. Ana almost forgot what she'd meant to say. "Yes, I talked to her on the radio. She invited me. Aren't you glad to see me?"

Instead of speaking, he put his other hand against her neck, his touch gentle against the fading bruises. "You know I am. But after all you've been through, I wasn't sure—I thought maybe you'd be eager to get back to the safety of the city."

Ana looked past him to the thick greenery of the rain forest. "When I watched the medics hooking my dad up to the IV, I thought about what your mother said—there could be lifesaving medicines out there, and we're wiping them out. I'd like to do a little to help, that's all. And I wanted to see you again, Brad. In the jungle, on top of a mountain—I'd feel safe anywhere with you beside me."

"We make a good team. I take back everything I said about you, city girl," Brad told her. "You're very special, Ana Puentes. Ever think of applying to UCLA?"

"Convince me." Ana smiled up at him. He leaned closer.

His lips were as firm and as warm as she remembered. His kiss made her heart beat fast. Was that a monkey shrieking, or just her own ears ringing? Ana felt perfectly in tune with the wilderness around them. Paradise was indeed in the eye of the beholder, she mused. And her paradise was right here in Brad's arms.

Author's Note

We can help our environment and our world by conserving resources like water and electricity and recycling at home. If you'd like to find out more about how to save the rain forest, contact an international conservation organization such as the World Wildlife Fund, 1250 Twenty-fourth Street, NW, Washington, DC 20037.